# MIGHT OF THE DRAGON

## A DRAGON FANTASY ADVENTURE

JASMINE WALT

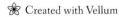 Created with Vellum

ONE

Life has a funny way of tricking you into thinking it's changed, when in reality things are exactly the same as they always were.

When I first became a dragon rider, when I laid hands on Lessie's egg and brought her into the world, I thought my life had been turned upside down. Before Lessie, I'd been a treasure hunter, former thief, and antique shop owner trying to get out from underneath Salcombe's shadow to stand on my own two feet. After Lessie, I became a rider, beholden to the state of Elantia, and yet freer in some ways than I'd ever been. For the first time, I'd felt a sense of home. I'd had a roof over my head, friends that I could count on, and the best companion in the world—a dragon I could conquer the skies with.

And yet, just a few short months later, I was back where I started. Perhaps not at the Treasure Trove authenticating objects, or out in the field looking for new artifacts, but I was back all the same. Under Salcombe's thumb again, in a foreign country, with no friends or dragon to help me escape his machinations.

And, as in the old times, we were on a hunt.

"You know," I said, a little annoyed as the carriage bumped and jostled along the road. We were on our way to a garden party hosted by the governor of Puilin, Traggar's capital city and the home of the royal family. "My treasure sense works on objects of value, not people. I don't see why you have to drag me to this garden party."

Salcombe merely arched an eyebrow at me. "And leave you home alone, so you can rummage through the house and figure out how to escape? I don't think so. I've trained you to use your eyes and ears, Zara, not only your treasure sense. You'll keep them both finely tuned as we socialize with the other partygoers, and together we will ferret out Lord Fanuel's location."

I scowled. *As if I'd be alone in the house,* I grumbled to myself. Salcombe had several bodyguards, including the oaf Trolbos who sat next to me in the carriage and took up *far* too much room on the bench. His menacing presence was never welcome, but the added insult of his huge thigh pressed up against my silken skirts made it even worse. He, or one of the others, was always posted in my quarters, barely giving me any room to breathe.

I smoothed down my skirts, wishing I had trousers to wear underneath. But Salcombe hadn't ordered anything so practical —these skirts and stays were meant to be trappings that would slow me down, another obstacle to slipping out the window in the middle of the night or making a break for it when we went out in public, like to this stupid party.

The carriage rolled to a halt outside a gate, and I let out a silent sigh of relief as the door opened, providing me an escape from Trolbos. Taking the waiting footman's hand, I stepped out into the night and took in a deep breath of fresh air. It was a bit chilly, and I tugged the wrap my maid had given me a bit tighter around my shoulders as I waited for Salcombe to disembark.

"Come, darling," Salcombe said, taking my arm in his. He looked every bit the dashing Warosian nobleman, the magic fan he'd surreptitiously bought from my shop smoothing the lines away from his normally haggard face, adding sparkle to his eyes, and darkening his thinning silver hair to thick, chocolate brown.

Briefly, I wondered if this was what Salcombe had looked like as a younger man. He was already old when I'd first come to him, a starving kid who'd tried to put food in her belly by stealing from the rich, and he'd taken me in to groom me as his own personal thief, treasure hunter, and occasional spy. Had he been so cynical and mercenary even in his youth? Or had something happened to make him this way?

Arm in arm, we approached the gate, appearing every inch the rich nobles from Warosia here in Traggar to indulge Salcombe's passion for history and relics. Salcombe produced an invitation from his waistcoat pocket and handed it to the guard, who looked it over with a keen eye.

"Lord and Lady Trentiano," he said, stepping aside so we could pass. "Welcome to Callentry Garden."

We walked through the gates together, past the high walls that surrounded the garden, and I felt no small amount of satisfaction that Trolbos was forced to remain behind with the carriage. *Garden* might have been a bit of a misnomer—several acres of land sprawled before us, the flora rigorously landscaped with clusters of flowering bushes and trees, arbors and benches, and flower beds boasting all manner of colorful blossoms. At least three hundred guests were present, their jewel-toned gowns and suits gleaming in the light from strategically placed gas lamps as they flirted and gossiped. Servers milled about, passing through the crowd with trays of wine and finger food, while chefs worked tirelessly to feed the guests at stations set up near long buffet tables.

My treasure sense immediately lit up at the sight of all that wealth, and the sound of conversation was instantly drowned out by a cacophony of chimes. Deliberately, I turned down the volume—the women here dripped with jewelry, and it would only distract me from our mission.

Not that I particularly wanted to succeed.

As Salcombe and I immersed ourselves in the crowd, mingling with the other nobles and socialites, we discreetly scanned the crowd, looking for Lord Jamison Fanuel. Fanuel was a famous, yet elusive, Traggaran mage, and Salcombe was convinced that he was descended from one of the five mages who had subdued Zakyiar, the fearsome dragon god who had nearly destroyed our world with his horde of dragons. Unable to be killed by mortal means, the only way to vanquish the dragon god had been to take his heart and split it into five pieces. Those pieces had been carefully hidden by the mages, who had changed their family names multiple times and disappeared from history so no one might find those pieces and resurrect the World Eater from his shadowy grave.

Unfortunately, Salcombe had managed to get his hands on one of those five pieces, and the dragon god now had his claws in him. My old mentor was obsessed, driven by madness and a hunger for power, and would do whatever it took to get his hands on the remaining pieces.

*Including forcing his foster daughter to help him by threatening her dragon's life,* I thought bitterly. Because if Salcombe killed me, Lessie would also die. And while I was willing to risk my own life, hers was another matter entirely. She was still a baby, only a few months old, and I hated the idea of her life being snuffed out after waiting so long for the right rider to hatch for. Her egg had been laid nearly three hundred years ago, and after two centuries of lying dormant, Tavarian's ancestors had deemed the egg a dud and locked it up in the family vault. The same vault I'd broken into, looking for Tavarian's piece of the dragon god's heart and finding Lessie instead.

I still didn't understand why Lessie had chosen me out of the hundreds of dragon riders that had been paraded before her in the past. But she was mine, and I hers, and I would do whatever it took to protect her. My heart ached fiercely at our separation—it had been over a week since I'd sent her back across the Traggaran channel and to the safety of Elantia—and I had to put her out of my mind before someone noticed my plummeting mood. Much as I hated it, I was here to play the part of Salcombe's wife, and I couldn't afford to slip up.

An hour into the party, my feet ached in the stupid heeled shoes Salcombe had forced me to wear—all the harder to run in

—and we'd still seen no sign of Lord Fanuel. I was about to try convincing Salcombe to leave when he fell into discussion with a trio of older scholars who seemed to be somewhat acquainted with the man we sought. Unfortunately for Salcombe, the men seemed more interested in me than him, ignoring his efforts to steer the conversation.

"Go amuse yourself elsewhere," he finally muttered in my ear when one of them turned to snag drinks from a passing server. "I am getting nowhere with you around—these men clearly prefer the sight of your bosom to scholarly discussion."

I had to stifle a smirk at the disgust in Salcombe's voice—he despised men who allowed their carnal urges to cloud their judgment. "Are you sure?" I whispered back. "I could probably use my charms to convince them to tell us anything you wanted." I batted my lashes at him for effect.

But Salcombe narrowed his eyes at me. "Get going," he hissed. "I will not allow you to derail my efforts."

*Dammit.* As usual, Salcombe saw right through me. "Excuse me, gentlemen," I said with a sweet smile. "It has been lovely talking to you, but I must seek out a friend who has been waiting for me."

I slipped away before the men could protest, drifting through the crowd. The moment I was away from Salcombe, worries crowded in on my mind again. It had been over a week since Lessie and I had last spoken, and though I could sense her through the bond, I couldn't communicate with her now. Had she gone back to the military camp, as I'd told her to? She'd still been injured when I'd forced her to leave, and I hated the idea of her hiding out somewhere alone, away from help.

*I wish I could get out of here,* I thought sourly as I looked around. I didn't belong with these nobles strutting around in the gardens, showing off their finery like preening peacocks as they tittered and gossiped with one another. I would slash my watered silk gown to ribbons if I could trade it for a pair of leathers and boots. Salcombe had even taken my spelled boots—ferreted away while I was in the bath—so I couldn't sneak about the house unheard. He was taking no chances, and since he was still in possession of my hair, which he could use to track me with a spell he'd purchased from a mage, I wouldn't get very far if I tried to run.

But even if I were to leave this place, what would I do? I'd been certain Lord Tavarian, my dragon rider sponsor and Elantia's unofficial ambassador, would be at this party, since every bigwig in the area had been invited. But I'd been scanning the crowd since I'd arrived and hadn't seen any sign of him. Could King Zoltar have imprisoned him after all? I wished there was someone I could ask, but I didn't dare draw any suspicion to myself. I'd already narrowly escaped a hanging once because the Traggarans had thought I was an Elantian spy—there was no reason to tempt fate again.

Suddenly tired of the crowds, I snatched a flute of champagne from a passing server, then retreated to a stone bench beneath a star blossom-laden tree. The heady scent of the spicy-sweet flowers surrounded me like a fragrant blanket, and I let out a silent sigh of relief when no one sat down next to me. After days of being watched by either Salcombe or one of his henchmen, it was nice to finally have a moment alone, and the hedges and bushes strategically placed around the tree certainly provided a sense of seclusion.

Unfortunately, I was only alone for a brief moment before a man sat down next to me. Annoyed, I twisted around to tell him to buzz off—in the politest tone possible—but the words froze in my throat.

"My lady." Lord Tavarian, looking as handsome and mysterious as ever in a suit of midnight blue, inclined his head. His silver eyes gleamed in the lamplight as he looked down at me— even seated he towered over me by at least a foot, and I wasn't a short woman. "I saw you sitting here, all on your own, and couldn't help but think it was a shame that such a lovely woman should be looking so lonesome at an event like this. Would you tell me your name?"

Aware that there were eyes on us—the hedge didn't completely obscure the bench—I gave him a flirtatious smile and offered my hand. "Lady Zara Trentiano," I said with a coy smile, as if my heart wasn't pounding a mile a minute in my chest. "Wife of Lord Trentiano. And you are...?"

Tavarian's eyes flickered at the mention of my "husband," and I wondered if he knew I was here with Salcombe. How long had he been at the party? Had he been watching me from some shadowed corner? "Lord Varrick Tavarian, at your service."

He lifted my hand to his mouth, and a shiver rippled through me as he brushed his warm lips against my skin. For a moment, I wondered what it would be like if we really were two strangers at a garden party indulging in a bit of flirtation. Would Tavarian tug me behind the hedges for a scandalous kiss? Or more? When I'd first met him, I couldn't have fathomed him to be the kind of man who would engage in a clandestine activity like that, especially in public, but sitting here now, with his lips on my skin, it was all too easy to imagine.

But when he lifted his head again, the look in his eyes destroyed all thoughts of intimacy. They were not the eyes of a man who wanted to sweep a woman into his arms and make her forget about everything but the way he made her feel.

They were the eyes of a man who was furious.

"I thought it was a mistake when I saw you enter the party on that man's arm," Tavarian said in a low voice. "Is that Salcombe, in disguise? And what are you doing here with him?"

"Yes," I hissed, annoyed now at his reaction. "It's a long story, but Lessie and I ended up in a storm that left us stranded here on the island. She was too injured to fly back with both of us, so I sent her on her way before a group of idiot villagers killed us both, and made my way to the capital to look for you. But before I could find you, I was arrested as an Elantian spy. I would have been executed if Salcombe hadn't whisked me out of the prison."

"And now he has you posing as his wife," Tavarian said softly. The spark of anger had disappeared, leaving behind the smooth, expressionless mask he usually presented to the world.

Tavarian turned his gaze to the garden, spotting Salcombe, who was still in deep discussion with the men I'd left him with. "What is he doing here with you?" he asked. "Surely he didn't bring you to this party for fun."

"He is looking for a mage by the name of Fanuel," I told him. "He seems convinced that Fanuel knows where one of the pieces of the dragon god's heart is. I need to get away from him before he can force me to locate it for him. Can you help?"

Tavarian sighed. "I wish I could, but I am as much a prisoner as you."

I struggled to hide my frown. "Just what is that supposed to mean?" He was here, dressed in fancy clothes and enjoying the same fancy food and company as everyone else. "Do you have thuggish bodyguards shadowing your every move as well?"

"'Bodyguard' is not the word for it," Tavarian said, his tone grim. "King Zoltar does not trust me in the slightest. He has refused to receive me even though I have been here for weeks, and I am constantly watched by strategically placed counterespionage agents he thinks I do not notice. Yesterday, I narrowly avoided an assassination attempt."

"*What?*" I barely managed to stop myself from shouting the word. "How?"

"A servant tried to slip poison into my soup," he said dryly. "Luckily, I have a discreet spell that I use to test my food whenever I travel abroad, and I was able to detect it. The constable was called, but since I am out of favor with the local government, the worst I could do to the girl was fire her."

"That's terrifying," I said, thinking back to the servants in Salcombe's hired townhouse. They were locals, too. Were any of them plants, sent by the king, or someone from his court, to spy on us? I wondered if Salcombe had thought of the possibility and taken appropriate precautions.

"It is," Tavarian agreed. "And there will be more attempts, I am certain. The military authorities and the weapons manufacturers they work with are the ones after me, not the king himself. They feel they must prevent me from speaking with him at all costs, as they do not want me averting either the war or the alliance. The way things are going right now, it does not look like the king plans on changing his mind about the impending war. The only reason that war has not been declared already is because Zoltar does not care for the Zallabarian ambassador. He is a bit on the stuffy side and rather conservative, while the king is blatantly hedonistic, so Zoltar takes great pleasure in making him wait. But it is only a matter of days before he formally pledges his troops to Zallabar, and if that happens, I will either be imprisoned or exiled."

"Shit."

Tavarian arched a brow. "That's not a very ladylike thing to say."

Remembering myself, I pasted another coy smile on my lips, picking up the flirtatious act once more. "Jokes, at a time like this?" I said lightly.

He smiled, just a little. "I find that a bit of levity helps in situations like this. I have been through worse, Zara. I am far more concerned about you. If push comes to shove, and I am forced to leave, I will try my best to take you with me. But as much as it pains me to say it, under the current circumstances you may actually be safer with Salcombe. Several innocent countrymen suspected of being Elantian spies have already been hanged, including a bookshop owner who was an old friend of mine." His eyes deepened with sorrow. "He emigrated from Elantia nearly twenty years ago to marry a Traggaran woman he'd fallen in love with, and left a large family behind. If someone like him, with deep roots in the community, can be executed, then I could easily be next."

My stomach plummeted as an image of Tavarian dangling from the gallows, his face bloated and bluish-purple in death, burst into my mind. But before I could say anything, he rose. "We have tarried too long," he murmured, and my chest tightened as I noticed Salcombe now staring in our direction. "Stay safe, Zara."

And with that, he disappeared, leaving me with the solitude I'd desperately craved, yet no longer wanted.

TWO

Painfully aware that Salcombe was watching me, I forced myself to get up from the bench and mingle with the crowd, careful not to go anywhere near Lord Tavarian. Had Salcombe recognized him? It *was* dark out, and we were far away, partially hidden by the hedges. It was entirely possible Salcombe hadn't seen him at all.

As the minutes passed, and it became apparent that Salcombe was not going to seek me out to pester me about my encounter, I relaxed. Clearly, he was not concerned. Perhaps he thought I was merely chatting up another nobleman in the hopes of ferreting out Lord Fanuel's location, like the good little soldier I'd been for so many years.

*Maybe I should socialize,* I thought as I picked at a small plate of fruit and cheese. Just because I didn't want to help Salcombe with his agenda didn't mean there wasn't valuable information to be gained here. I might be able to learn something that would help Tavarian with his mission. After all, if he could convince the Traggarans to back down before Salcombe whisked me out of the capital, there was a chance I could go back to Elantia with him.

The thought of getting away from Salcombe and reuniting with Lessie lit a fire under me, and for the next hour, I wholeheartedly threw myself into the party. Most of the attendees were Traggaran nobles, not particularly known for their hospitality to outsiders, especially ones who did not speak their language well. But I could be charming when I wanted. I focused most of my attention on the men, who I knew would have a hard time resisting the smiles and attentions of a young, pretty woman. It worked well enough—though the women didn't much appreciate it—but I didn't find out anything useful, mages or otherwise. Every time I brought up the subject of magic, the Traggarans recoiled with distaste. Their general attitude was that mages were dangerous, best to be avoided. No one I spoke to had heard of Lord Fanuel, which made me think they practiced what they preached even amongst their own circle.

*Well that's something,* I told myself. If the Traggaran nobles refused to associate with Fanuel, that would make him that much harder for Salcombe to find.

As I made my rounds through the various clusters of guests, I noticed one man who spoke with a heavy Zallabarian accent. "Excuse me, sir," I said in perfect Zallabarian, recognizing the crest embroidered onto his very expensive-looking tunic. "Are you the Zallabarian ambassador?"

He turned to me, a look of surprised delight on his face. "I am. General Trattner, at your service. And who might you be?"

"Lady Zara Trentiano," I said with a smile. "My husband

and I are from Warosia, but my mother-in-law is Zallabarian, and we travel there quite often." In fact, that was how Salcombe had managed to get his false Zallabarian citizenship papers—by faking a relative. "It is a pleasure to meet someone else from my mother-in-law's home country."

"And it is a pleasure to meet you," he said, inclining his head. "Your Zallabarian is impeccable. If not for your surname, I would never have guessed you were not a native."

The two of us exchanged a few words of polite conversation, and though the ambassador did not seem like the type to normally indulge pretty young girls in conversation—he was, as Tavarian had warned, a bit on the stuffy side—I managed to reel him in by talking to him about Zallabarian history. I'd been to Zallabar several times on treasure hunts, and that, combined with my recent study of the nation in preparation for the war, made me quite well-versed in their history and culture. In no time at all, we were walking around the garden, arm in arm, discussing the pre-dragon war exploits of past Zallabarian kings.

"I must admit I did not expect to enjoy your company quite so much," Trattner said as we stopped by one of the refreshment tables to grab a bite of food. "Most of the men here have little interest in discussing learned subjects such as history, never mind the history of my own country. They much prefer to talk of gossip, or hunting, or whatever frivolous pursuits have currently struck their fancy."

The hint of distaste in his voice told me that the Zallabarian ambassador liked the Traggarans about as much as King Zoltar liked him. "The Traggarans do take a bit of effort to warm up to," I said, giving him a sympathetic pat on the forearm. "But I am sure that they will become much friendlier once you have finalized the alliance. After all, they have been wanting to go after Elantia for decades, have they not?"

"Indeed, but it seems that Traggarans take things at a slower pace than we Zallabarians do. Adjusting to this...leisurely attitude of war has been a challenge, to say the least," Trattner said, his tone crackling with frustration. I held my breath, hoping he would say more, but he blinked, seeming to realize what he had said. "Forgive me, my lady. I did not mean to sour the mood with such talk."

"It's no trouble at all," I said soothingly, moving in a bit closer. "I am always willing to lend an ear to a friend."

He smiled. "You remind me of my wife," he said. His eyes, a clear gray, softened with wistfulness. "I wish I could have brought her with me. She is a devoted historian, and our four children are also quite passionate about learning. I believe she would have greatly enjoyed conversing with you."

"I am sure I would have as well," I said, surreptitiously leaning away from him. The hint was clear—he was a family man, devoted to his wife, and I definitely had no desire to overstep any boundaries. "Speaking of spouses, I really should be getting back to my husband. He will be wondering where I have gotten off to."

"Of course." Gently, he extricated his arm from mine and gave my hand a quick squeeze. "It was lovely to meet you, Lady Zara. If we should find ourselves at the same event and you are in need of good conversation, please feel free to seek me out."

I slipped away and rejoined Salcombe, who stood near a fountain talking to a matron who seemed far more interested in flirting than she was in answering Salcombe's questions. The relief on Salcombe's face when he saw me approaching was almost palpable, and for a split second I thought about veering off in another direction, if only to make him sweat a little.

But I didn't want to provoke Salcombe, so I returned to his side like the dutiful wife I was pretending to be.

"Darling," I cooed, leaning my head on his shoulder. "I find I am afflicted with a terrible headache. Can we retire for the evening?"

"How terrible," Salcombe said, putting his arm around me. He gave a perfunctory smile to the woman, who was eyeing me with annoyance. "Excuse me, my lady, but my wife is feeling under the weather. I must escort her home now."

As we walked toward the gate, I spotted Lord Tavarian off to the side, talking with an older man in military uniform. I did my best not to look directly at him, but from the way Salcombe's grip tightened on my arm, I knew he'd spotted him.

"It seems you have been quite busy tonight," he murmured in my ear. "Did Lord Tavarian have anything of interest to say when you cozied up to him on the bench?"

*Dammit.* He *had* seen. "The conversation was disappointing," I said in a clipped voice. "He told me that I would be safer staying with you and to keep out of his way." There. That wasn't even a lie.

Salcombe smirked. "He's not wrong," he said as we passed through the gates, stopping at the curb to wait for our carriage. "Lord Tavarian could be murdered or thrown out of the country any day now. He couldn't even save that friend of his from hanging, and if he loses his diplomatic status he may very well suffer the same fate. He is certainly in no position to help *you*."

I glowered at Salcombe, forgetting that I had resolved not to provoke him. "You sound like you want him to be disgraced."

"And why wouldn't I?" Salcombe asked. "If not for him, I wouldn't have to threaten you to keep you by my side. Tavarian is an obstacle, especially since he is protecting a piece of the dragon god's heart, and under different circumstances I might try to eliminate him myself. But there is no need to put myself at risk when the Traggarans are doing such a good job at keeping him at bay."

I pressed my lips together, deciding not to mention that if Salcombe hadn't sent me to Tavarian's estate to steal the piece of heart, I never would have met him. The carriage pulled up, and Trolbos exited and held the door.

"All the same," Salcombe said when we were settled inside, "I forbid you from meeting with Lord Tavarian again, should we run into him at future gatherings. If I were to find out that you are conspiring with him against me, it would take very little effort to whisper into the right ear and have him thrown into the very dungeons I rescued you from."

My blood turned to ice. "Don't worry," I said stiffly. "I have no use for him, since he can't help me anyway."

Salcombe chuckled. "Good. You are learning."

Trolbos settled back into the carriage again, this time next to Salcombe. I held in a sigh as he fixed me with a glare, and looked out the window, trying to ignore him. The party had given me a brief respite from the hulking giant, but now that I was back in his vicinity, his animosity was greater than ever. He clearly didn't like being forced to wait outside, away from his employer, unable to keep an eye on me while I was getting up to who knew what. I was relieved when the carriage finally rolled to a stop outside our rented townhouse and I was able to put some distance between us.

Back inside the townhouse, Salcombe and I adjourned to the sitting room, where a servant had set out tea and biscuits. The last thing I wanted was to spend more time with Salcombe, but I forced myself to join him on the sofa, stirring a cube of sugar and some cream into my cup. I wanted him to let his guard down, to start seeing me as a partner rather than a prisoner, and in order to do that I had to at least appear cooperative.

"Did those scholars you were talking to give you any useful information?" I asked.

"No," Salcombe admitted, "but one of them did introduce me to the king's high chancellor, who has promised to present us at court next week."

"Court?" My mind froze as I struggled to process what to many was considered a great honor. "Don't I need to have a fancy dress or something?"

"You do," Salcombe said dryly. "The fanciest dress you are likely to ever wear in your lifetime, even to your own wedding, should you ever marry. You will go to the modiste first thing tomorrow to be fitted."

"I doubt she'll be able to have something ready for me on such short notice," I protested. "And a week isn't nearly long enough to prepare. What if we accidentally blow our cover? If they find out that we're not actually Warosian nobles, they'll have us hanged as spies."

"I will let the modiste be the judge of whether or not a week is long enough to make such a dress," Salcombe said. "As far as blowing our cover, that is not a concern. I have been preparing for this meeting much longer than you have. So long as you look pretty and keep your mouth shut, there is no reason anything should go wrong."

I swallowed a nasty retort—Salcombe hadn't raised me to be pretty and docile, but intelligent and effective. The fact that he now expected me to pretend to be a china doll chafed, but I'd already objected too much, so I kept my thoughts to myself. Maybe I could find a way to turn our court visit to my advantage.

Salcombe seemed to misinterpret the look on my face as anxiety, as his expression softened. "I have not prepared you for this kind of thing," he said, "so I have arranged for Lady Astilla Denham to assist you over the next few days. She is an upstanding member of Traggaran high society, dull enough that she won't ask the wrong questions, but with the right connections to make sure you get everything you need."

"I see." I pasted a grateful smile on my face. "Is there anything I can do to help you in the meantime?"

Salcombe shook his head. "I will spend the next few days in a private library one of the scholars I spoke to offered me access to, while you get ready for court. Hopefully, I will be able to unearth a few more clues about the remaining heart pieces."

"All right." I set my tea cup down and rose. "Since I'll likely have to make an early start of it tomorrow, I'll be going to bed now."

"Zara." Salcombe's voice stopped me before I managed to

make it more than two steps. I turned back to see him staring at me, his brow furrowed. "I saw you flirting with General Trattner, the Zallabarian ambassador."

"What of it?" My stomach tensed. Was there something about the ambassador I didn't know? Was he an enemy of Salcombe's? If so, maybe I could exploit it.

But Salcombe merely looked annoyed, not agitated. "I know I told you to go amuse yourself, but do not waste your time talking to foreigners. They are of no use to us on our current quest."

"Actually, it turns out that the ambassador has an interest in history and antiquities," I said. "It's quite possible he might prove to be a useful connection in the future."

Salcombe thought it over. "I suppose you have a point," he finally said. "Very well, you may continue to foster the relationship. Good night."

I went off to my room, chewing over everything I'd learned tonight. That last exchange with Salcombe proved he was thinking long-term and didn't have plans to kill me anytime soon, despite his threats. Indeed, even though he was still focused on getting the pieces of the dragon god's heart, he didn't seem quite as obsessive as he had the first time he'd kidnapped me. Could it be that the dragon god's influence on him was lessening, due to decreased proximity to the heart?

*Careful, Zara,* I warned myself as the maid helped me out of my clothes and into a nightgown. It would do no good for me to fall into the trap of thinking Salcombe could be redeemed. He was my adversary, regardless of our history, and he needed to be stopped.

Depression settled heavily on my chest as I slid into bed. I was in enemy territory, at Salcombe's mercy, without a single friend to turn to for help. Even Tavarian was of no help to me—until he got his audience with the Traggaran king, he couldn't make a single move without risking his own neck. I was on my own.

Desperate for comfort, I reached through the bond for Lessie, wanting reassurance that she was still alive. The moment I did, I felt a surge of anger so strong it stole my breath. Heart pounding, I shot upright in bed, straining to reach her across the bond. What was happening?

*"Lessie? Are you there? What's wrong?"*

But Lessie didn't answer. All I could feel was her anger, mixed with a healthy dose of frustration. Something had *really* pissed her off. I clenched my fists, growing angry as well. I'd sent Lessie back to camp because I'd thought the military would protect her. If anything happened while she was in their custody...

*Calm down,* I ordered before I worked myself into a frenzy. Lessie might be angry, but she wasn't afraid, or sad, or anxious. Whatever was going on wasn't life-threatening. She might not even be at camp at all. Biting my lip, I wondered how things were going on the other side of the channel. The soldiers were all aware that I was AWOL by now...were they worried for me, or had they branded me as a deserter? I was almost certain that Colonel Roche, who'd hated me from the start, assumed the worst about my absence. But perhaps Lessie had returned and explained to the other dragons what had happened. Kadryn would definitely pass that information on to Jallis, but would he do anything with it? He seemed so reluctant to stick up for me lately that I honestly had no idea what he'd do.

Helpless, I tried to push as much affection as I could through the bond, trying to let Lessie know I was thinking about her and that I'd get back to her as soon as I could. The best I could hope for was that she received the message, and that it would calm her.

*Shut it off, Zara,* I ordered myself. But Lessie was as much a part of me as my beating heart. And now that I'd felt her pain, I could no more shut it off than I could stop breathing.

THREE

I'd hoped that Lessie's anger would abate the next morning, but when I awoke after only three hours of sleep, I could still feel her volatile emotions. Her frustration stirred my own, and I actually threw a pillow at the maid who was trying to drag me out of bed.

"Go away," I grumbled. "I'm still sleeping!"

"It's nearly eleven in the morning," the maid said. She tugged at the coverlet, and it came off in one motion. Groaning, I curled myself into a ball and did my best to ignore the draft tickling my legs. "Your appointment with the modiste is in two hours. Lord Trentiano has ordered me to make sure you are ready, so you must get up!"

Crap. I'd already forgotten about that. If Salcombe found out I'd missed my appointment with the dressmaker with only a week to go until we were to be presented at court, he'd skin me alive. Maybe literally. Wide awake, I jumped out of bed and ripped my nightshift over my head.

"Dress me," I said to the now wide-eyed maid.

The maid did so, sticking me in a gown of robin's egg blue and piling my curls into a half-up, half-down look that was somehow elegant and messy all at once. Tiny blue gems were fastened at my ears, but the rest of me was unadorned aside from the faux wedding band Salcombe forced me to wear at all times. Even though I hated being dragged out of bed before I was ready, I had to admit that I never would have been able to make myself presentable without the maid's help. She, along with the rest of the household staff, belonged to the noble who owned the house. From what I understood, he was renting it out because he'd been banished from court. Apparently the man had inadvertently insulted the king's sense of style, and had been forced to flee the capital before the king jailed him.

*And I have to meet this guy in a week?* I grumbled to myself. I'd better let Salcombe do the talking if King Zoltar addressed us. I wasn't sure I'd be able to hold my tongue, knowing the guy was a despot who treated women like chattel, and as a foreigner I'd receive even harsher treatment than a local if I offended the king in any way.

I was just entering the dining area for a late breakfast when Willsworth, the butler, stuck his head in through another door. "Lady Astilla is here to see you, my lady."

Already? Damn. "Please, invite her in," I said. "You can tell her she's welcome to join me for a late breakfast if she hasn't had anything to eat yet."

I was just about to bite into a freshly buttered slice of toast when the woman bustled into the room, hands aflutter. She was mid-thirties, blonde, with excellent bone structure and a face that would have been quite pleasant to look at if her blue eyes weren't bulging out of her skull as she rushed toward me.

"Lady Zara!" she cried, knocking the bread from my hands. "You mustn't eat that!"

My heart jumped into my throat. "Why?" Was it poisoned?

"Because you're about to go to a fitting, of course!" She looked at me as though I'd lost my mind. "The modiste won't be able to measure you accurately if your stomach is bloated from all that food!"

I raised an eyebrow, glancing down at the forlorn piece of toast on my plate. "I'm not convinced that a single piece of bread and butter is going to spoil my figure, Lady Astilla. Besides, if the modiste is off by an inch or so in my waist, that merely means I won't suffocate to death if I end up going to dinner in this dress."

"This is your *presentation* dress," Lady Astilla said. She sounded utterly flabbergasted. "You won't be wearing it for any other occasion!"

"Even so," I said firmly, "this toast and I have a date, and it will not be delayed any further."

To Lady Astilla's consternation, I ate not one but *three* slices of toast, liberally slathered in jam and butter. I would have happily added ham and eggs to my plate if we'd had time for a proper breakfast, but I *had* gotten up late, and I didn't actually want to stuff myself right before a fitting. I could always eat afterward, I told myself.

"All right," I said, setting down my napkin. "I am ready to go."

"It's about time," Lady Astilla said. "Fetch your parasol so we may be off."

*Parasol?* I almost blurted out, then thought better of it. Anyone could surmise by the healthy color in my skin that I wasn't the type who stayed out of the sun, but carrying a parasol was the proper thing to do, and I didn't need to tip the lady off about my uncouth upbringing.

I went back upstairs to my room to fetch said parasol, plus a small coin purse Salcombe had given me for incidentals. This went into my skirt pocket, along with a small steak knife that I had filched from the dining table a few nights ago. It was no dragon blade, but it would have to do until I could steal my stuff back from Salcombe.

When I came back down to the foyer, Lady Astilla was already waiting for me. "Let's be off," she said, a little impatiently. "We don't want to be late!"

"Hang on." I turned to Willsworth. "Where is Trolbos?"

"He is with Lord Trentiano today," the butler said. "Your husband thought that you and Lady Astilla would enjoy your outing better if it was just you ladies today."

"Too right he is," Lady Astilla said. "It is admirable that your husband worries for your safety, but you are perfectly safe at my side, traveling through the city in broad daylight. It is not as if we are going into the seedy parts of town, after all, and a manservant is hardly necessary for a trip to the modiste."

I swallowed a grin as I followed Lady Astilla out to the waiting carriage. It had to chap Trolbos's ass that he couldn't follow me around today, but Salcombe was right. Walking around with that big brute over my shoulder would draw too much attention. He was just going to have to rely on the threats he'd made against me and my friends to keep me from running off.

Willsworth helped the two of us into the carriage, and Lady Astilla smoothed the lilac skirts of her dress as she sat on the bench across from me. "Well, this is quite exciting," she said as the carriage lurched into motion. "Your very first presentation at court! Are you nervous?"

"A little," I admitted. "I've never done this before."

Lady Astilla's eyes widened. "Never? You never had your debut when you were in Warosia? Surely your father would have presented you to the court there!"

*Crap.* I hid a wince. "Oh, no, of course he did," I said hastily. I'd forgotten that countries with monarchies did that sort of thing amongst their elite. Did the Elantian nobles have a similar custom? I'd grown up on the streets, so I had no way of knowing. "I only meant that I've never been presented at court in a strange country. I don't know the customs."

"Don't you worry." Lady Astilla patted my hand in a motherly fashion. "I promised your husband that I would help you practice. There is a strict set of rules regarding how one is to be presented at court, but I am confident that we can get you ready in a week's time."

I swallowed. "What kind of rules?"

But Lady Astilla waved her hand. "We can discuss all that after your fitting," she said, sounding unconcerned.

"But—"

"This is a very exciting time to be visiting court, don't you think?" Lady Astilla went on, completely ignoring me. "His upcoming marriage is certainly shaking things up."

"Marriage?" My brain switched gears. "But I thought the king was already married."

"Oh, he is." Lady Astilla's eyes sparkled with glee as she leaned in. "But the king is divorcing her, on account of the fact that she has failed to produce a son in the three years they've been married. The latest object of his affection, Lady Hariana, is actually one of the queen's former ladies-in-waiting. She's a mercenary little bitch," she added with a curl of her lip, "flaunting their relationship in front of everyone even though the king is still technically married."

"Sounds like it." I couldn't quite hide my own disgust. I had learned that King Zoltar was an unpleasant, capricious man who had little regard for the sanctity of marriage, but I hadn't realized it was *this* bad. "How many times has he been married?"

"If Lady Hariana succeeds, she will be his fourth." Lady Astilla smirked. "Though I don't imagine she will last very long. She is quite pretty, but her hips are on the narrow side. I wouldn't be surprised if she fails to provide the king with an heir either."

I shook my head. Was this really what the nobility was focused on, while war loomed on the horizon? But then again, Traggar was a conquering nation—they were always going to battle with some country or other. For the nobles, war was a natural part of life.

The carriage slowed as we got to the busier section of town, and I glanced out the window, trying to distract myself. My mouth dropped open as I found myself staring at an execution scaffold that had been set up in the middle of the square. Six bodies hung from the ropes, swaying in the morning breeze, their faces purple and bloated in death. That in itself would have been shocking enough, but what was next to it—

"Amazing, isn't it?" Lady Astilla said in a shocked whisper, leaning in to stare as well. Next to the scaffold, mounted on a pike, was the head of a dragon. Not just any dragon, I realized with dismay, but Hallus, my former patrol partner's mount. The last time I'd seen him, he and Carvin had been hurtling toward the ocean, struck out of the sky by a bolt of lightning. I'd thought they would have sunk to the bottom of the sea, eaten by fish, but this...

"Those dragon riders think they're so superior to us," Lady Astilla continued in a haughty tone, completely unaware of my distress. There were people crowded around Hallus's head, and the sight of them jeering and throwing rotting vegetables at it made my stomach turn. "And yet we were able to take this brute out of the sky quite easily with our cannons. We don't even have the newfangled ones the Zallabarians have invented. If the Elantians could see this now, they would think twice about going to war with Zallabar. The fact that they haven't surrendered already shows how foolish they are."

"Indeed," I said, my voice hollow. I knew the self-congratulatory story about the cannons was a load of crock—I'd been there when Hallus and his rider had been struck out of the sky by a bolt of lightning. We'd been in the midst of a storm so fierce that no one from below would have seen us even if they'd been near a cannon. It was far more likely that a group of fishermen recovered Hallus's body and brought it to the authorities for his head to be hacked off and displayed here.

Lady Astilla frowned. "Are you all right, Lady Zara? You look a bit peaky."

I cleared my throat and leaned back in my chair, away from the gruesome view. "I'm a bit shocked, that's all. It's not every day you see a dead body, never mind six in a row."

"Of course." Lady Astilla tugged the curtains closed, adopting a soothing tone. "I should have thought of this. You wouldn't be used to the public executions we do here."

I stared. "You mean this is normal?"

Lady Astilla laughed, but it was a strained sound, with an edge of fear. "It didn't use to be, but times have changed. We have a hanging at least once a week, sometimes two."

My blood ran cold, and once again, I was reminded of how close I'd come to being one of those bodies left swinging in the wind, life and dignity stripped from me. Anger surged in my chest, and I had to lock down my expression so Lady Astilla would not notice. I was sick of this country, sick of these people! And I was sick of the military, too. It was a mere stroke of luck that Hallus's head was on that pike rather than Lessie's—we could have been struck by that lightning instead. If only we hadn't flown into the storm, I wouldn't be stuck here in this carriage, amongst these bloodthirsty people who hid their brutality behind smiles and satin. The curtains might be blocking the view, but I could still hear the boos and shouted insults from the crowd outside.

Finally, the carriage moved forward, the traffic jam ahead unblocked. Lady Astilla chattered on about court gossip, but it was easy enough to tune her out—she seemed more than happy to talk *at* me rather than *with* me. It took another twenty minutes before we finally arrived at the establishment— Madame Ricci's Dress Shop.

"Your husband instructed that we were to purchase a full wardrobe for you while we are here," Lady Astilla gushed excitedly as we walked into the shop. The place was busy; women crowded around counters as the dressmakers showed them sketches and helped them select bolts of cloth and various trimmings for their gowns. "Once we are done here, we will visit the milliner, the shoemaker, and the jeweler. He is such a generous man to insist that we spare no expense, don't you think?"

"He certainly is," I said, biting my tongue to keep back the retort that sprang to my lips. Salcombe had rarely shown me generosity in his life—anytime he'd given me anything, he'd expected me to pay for it in some fashion or another. This wardrobe was another investment, nothing more. Schooling my features into a pleasant smile, I allowed Lady Astilla to lead me to the counter.

"Lady Zara Trentiano and Lady Astilla Denham," she announced to the rail-thin woman standing there. "We have an appointment."

"Ah, yes." The woman brightened, apparently recognizing the name. To my horror, she switched to Warosian. "My name is Madame Ricci. It is such a pleasure to have a fellow Warosian in the shop today!"

"Wonderful," I said, and tried not to cringe. I was fluent in Warosian, but I spoke it with an accent. "Do you have a catalogue I can look through?" I asked, switching back to Traggaran, which I was becoming fairly adept in now that I was forced to speak it every day. "I'm afraid I don't know what presentation dresses in Traggar are supposed to look like."

The modiste narrowed her eyes briefly, and my heart sped up. Was that suspicion? But she quickly covered it with a smile, then pushed a small binder toward me. "These are the basic designs."

I perused the sketches, trying to hide my dismay. All of the dresses had unwieldy hoops and ridiculously long trains. "Are those ostrich feathers?" I asked.

"Indeed," Lady Astilla said. "All ladies who are presented at court are required to follow a strict dress code." She passed her hand over a particularly ridiculous dress, the skirt enhanced with panniers so that it flared out wide on each side and appeared flattened in the front. "I think that would look quite nice on you."

"*That* is going to make me look like a box."

The modiste gave me a wry smile. "Perhaps you would prefer this one."

She flipped to a sketch of another gown, and I frowned as I studied it. Like the others, it still had the hoops and the ridiculous feathered headdress, but the skirt was more like a bell than a box, beginning at the waistline and flaring out until it touched the floor. The neckline was a V that exposed a healthy amount of décolletage, and the sleeves were short and puffy at the top.

But it was the decoration of the dress itself that caught my eye, for it did not feature flowers or abstract designs like many of the other dresses did. No, the skirt was embroidered with beautiful peacock feathers that swept from the middle of the skirt down to the hem and along the train.

I jabbed at the feathers. "Would it be possible to incorporate these into the bodice?" I asked. "Real ones? Like so." I traced my fingers over the bodice to show how the feathers would line up, their tips brushing over my chest and covering up that V-neck.

Lady Astilla frowned. "That is an unusual design for a presentation dress," she said. "The necklines are usually cut lower."

I raised an eyebrow. "Is pushing up one's breasts until they are in danger of spilling out at the top of one's dress a part of the presentation rules?"

The modiste exchanged a glance with the society matron, who likely was regretting this outing with every second that passed. "No," she said, the corners of her mouth quirking up in a smile. "I suppose it is not."

"Astilla!" a woman cried. A brunette in her mid-forties arrowed straight toward us, a girl of maybe seventeen at her side. "How lovely to see you!"

"Claria!" Lady Astilla exclaimed with delight. "Lady Zara, this is my friend, Lady Claria Thrain. Claria, this is Lady Zara Trentiano."

"Oooh, the wife of the mysterious Lord Trentiano, is it?" Claria's eyes gleamed as she sized me up. "You are quite a bit younger than I expected."

"I married well," I said simply, and she laughed.

A few more women came over to chat with Lady Astilla, and I listened to them with half an ear as I continued my session with the modiste, flipping through sketches so I could flesh out the rest of my wardrobe. Apparently, the relatives of the current queen were furious at the king, and might very well refuse to attend the coming reception where Salcombe and I were to be presented. Tensions were fraught at court, and, as with Lady Astilla, the women seemed to be more occupied with who was backstabbing whom than with the war.

At least, until they came to the subject of Tavarian.

"It is really too bad that the man is an Elantian," Claria said with feeling. "He is so handsome and distinguished, and clearly quite wealthy. He would make a fine husband, don't you think, Laia?" she said to her daughter.

"Never mind Laia," one of the other women said with a lascivious wink. "I would fancy taking a turn with him myself, I think!"

The women laughed, even as the daughter's cheeks turned a deep crimson. "Well, if you want to, you're going to have to move fast," Lady Astilla said. "With the way things are going, the only way you'll be able to visit him is at the gaol, if he is not kicked out of the country."

The conversation quickly moved away from the subject of Tavarian, but I was no longer listening, still stuck on his fate. I wondered what he would think if he knew the noble ladies were tittering about how handsome he was while simultaneously bemoaning his unfortunate circumstances. I wished there was some way I could help him prevent the war, but after everything I'd seen and heard so far, it was clearer than ever that I needed to put all my attention on playing my part convincingly.

"All right," Madame Ricci finally said, closing the binder. "I believe we are all set. Let's go into the back and take your measurements, shall we?"

"Yes," I said, with feeling. I was so sick of looking at dresses. Apparently, the few outfits Salcombe had furnished me with were not nearly enough for a lady of my supposed breeding. A proper lady required morning gowns, visiting gowns, walking gowns, promenade dresses, carriage dresses, dinner gowns, ball gowns, and riding habits. And that didn't include the various underpinnings required—shifts, chemises, stays, corsets, hoops, petticoats, stockings, and more! The list was endless, and I briefly wondered if Salcombe knew how much all of this was going to cost. Were we going to be here long enough for me to wear even half of these garments?

The modiste whisked me behind a curtain, where a team of ladies stripped me down to my chemise and measured me within an inch of my life. "So, which part of Warosia do you and your husband come from?" she said casually as she switched back to her native tongue.

I fought back my anger at the enterprising glint in the woman's eye—after all the money I was spending, she was still going to try and twist my arm? "I am not actually from Warosia," I said, giving her what I hoped was an apologetic smile. "I am from Ruisin, and I became acquainted with my husband through a family friend. When the two of us married, I naturally moved to Warosia to be with him."

"I see." But the modiste didn't seem convinced. "You should make sure that is well-understood, then. You wouldn't want someone to get the wrong idea and think you are a spy."

"I have nothing to fear on that end," I said airily, resisting the urge to punch the woman in her bony face. "My husband is a very important man with many friends here, and is fabulously rich. I'm sure he will have no problem at all when I tell him that I am doubling my order. Besides," I added, allowing a thread of steel to enter my voice, "I am sure that as a foreigner yourself, you would not want to let the authorities hear you talking of spies. They too might get the wrong idea."

The modiste stiffened, even as she gave me a wide smile. "That is wonderful news," she said, and I could tell that both my bribe and warning had hit the mark. "I will make sure everything is delivered well in advance."

I stared after her as she bustled away, a pit of unease growing in my stomach. How many more people would I have to cajole and bribe to look the other way? I sincerely hoped that Salcombe didn't intend for us to stay long, or we might soon find ourselves caught up in a trap even he couldn't weasel out of.

FOUR

The next week passed in a dizzying storm of activity. When I wasn't with Lady Astilla, practicing for my court presentation, I was being whisked off to all sorts of parties and dinners so Salcombe could continue to make connections and mine the guests for information. It never ceased to amaze me how often nobles got together for this sort of thing. Didn't they ever tire of it? It was exhausting to constantly primp and prep and fuss, spending evening upon evening engaging complete strangers in conversation. The whole thing was quite an education, and I quickly learned how to act like an aristocrat, mimicking their speech mannerisms and facial expressions, the way they could compliment someone so effusively in one moment, then cut them down in the next with a single word.

Even though I hated all the socializing, part of me was thankful to be kept busy. My separation from Lessie gnawed a hole in my heart, and whenever I was alone with my thoughts, I missed her terribly. I could confide in no one about my heartache—Salcombe would not sympathize in the least, and I couldn't very well tell General Trattner, whom I found myself spending more and more time with. We ran into each other often, running in similar social circles, and he was more than happy to answer my questions about various Zallabarian temples and sites under the pretext that I wanted to visit them.

"It is quite a shame that we are on the brink of war," he said to me as we sat in the salon at one of the many house parties I'd been invited to. "This is the perfect time of year for you to visit the northern temples—not too hot or too cold—but with dragons flying near our borders, I'm afraid it's too risky."

"Does either side have plans to strike soon?" I asked, widening my eyes. "From what I hear it seems that there have been a few skirmishes, but no official battles as of yet."

"I am not at liberty to discuss specifics," he said, "but it is only a matter of time. I will be meeting with King Zoltar at the reception, and the agreement will be signed the following morning."

*Dammit.* I wanted to probe the ambassador for more information, but I couldn't without arousing suspicion. Was there anything that could be done to stop the reception from happening, or stop the general from attending? I wished Tavarian were here, so I could speak with him, but he hadn't made an appearance at this particular gathering. In fact, I'd only seen him a handful of times since our encounter at the garden party.

"Is everything all right, Zara?" Salcombe asked in the carriage as we returned home. It was just the two of us—Trolbos had been left behind, as Salcombe couldn't very well bring his thugs to these parties, and in fact I was seeing less and less of him. My former mentor seemed to realize how uncomfortable Trolbos made me and responded by putting distance between the two of us. Salcombe subscribed to the idea that employees were more productive when their basic needs were met, so I tried not to read too much into it, and reminded myself that a man who was forcing me to do his bidding and who would not allow me access to my weapons or personal possessions was not, and could never be, my friend.

"Everything is fine," I lied, "except that we're getting nowhere with our search to find Lord Fanuel. I'm beginning to wonder if the man exists, or if he's just a myth. How much longer must we continue to put up with these toffs?"

I expected Salcombe to be annoyed with my outburst, but to my surprise, he gave me a sympathetic nod. "I too find these endless social rounds to be quite tedious," he said. "You know that I prefer my books and collections to the company of people. However"—his eyes gleamed—"I believe we are finally reaching the end of the road. There is a Lord Elliot Rycroft attending the king's reception—he is a cousin of Fanuel, and I am confident he will be able to give us the information we seek."

*We.* As if the two of us were a team. I had to hold back a scoff. "Do you really think that he'll just come out and tell us what we want to know?" I said, keeping up the charade that this was a willing partnership.

"There may be some resistance, but I have prepared for that." Salcombe sounded unconcerned. "The two of us will be wearing matching seal rings that contain a strong truth potion. It lowers inhibitions and inspires an irresistible urge to bare one's honest feelings and hold nothing back."

I narrowed my eyes. "You mean like the truth potion you and your cronies forced on me back in the airship?"

"I had to know if you were telling the truth, Zara," Salcombe said. "I knew the potion wouldn't harm you in any way. It isn't even the first time I used it on you."

My mouth fell open. *"Excuse me?"*

"When you were a child, I had to ensure you had not been sent to me as a spy by some rival before I took you in."

I ground my teeth but said nothing. After all, it wasn't as if I had come to Salcombe as an innocent. I'd broken into his house and tried to steal from him. It was only natural of him to be suspicious. And yet, I felt violated that he'd used the substance on me multiple times, against my will.

"I really hope you're right, and that this Rycroft can tell us where to find Fanuel," I finally said. "I'm not suited to this pretentious aristocracy we're pretending to be a part of. I have nothing in common with these people."

"That is the silliest thing I've ever heard you say," Salcombe said, and if I'd been sitting in a normal chair, I would have fallen right off it. "As the daughter of a dragon rider, you are more than equal to any of these foreign aristocrats. You too have an elite lineage."

Something about the way he said that made me pause. "Just how long have you known I had dragon rider blood?" I asked cautiously.

"Almost from the day you tried to rob me," Salcombe said with a faint smile. "Your treasure-hunting talent was a clear sign, and I had your background investigated. I know exactly who your parents were and where they came from."

The world seemed to tilt on its axis, and I stared at Salcombe, feeling betrayed all over again. "You never thought to tell me any of this?" I shouted, nearly lunging across the carriage. Emotion slammed into me so hard that I could hardly breathe. I wanted to grab Salcombe by the front of his coat and shake him until all the secrets he'd hidden from me came tumbling out of the crevices of his black heart. "Why would you hide such a thing from me?"

"Because your talent would have been wasted up there in the clouds," Salcombe snapped. "If I had revealed your true parentage, you would have been sent to live with your family and bred to become just like the toffs you so despise, forced to live in a box that never suited you. You may hate me, Zara, but you thrived under my tutelage. You never would have seen and done all the things you have if you'd been groomed as a dragon rider."

"You..." I trailed off, unable to come up with a proper retort. Salcombe was right, wasn't he? If Salcombe hadn't taken me in, I never would have become a treasure hunter. Thanks to his patronage, I'd visited many countries, learned about all sorts of fascinating cultures and history. I already knew from spending time at Dragon Rider Academy that I had an expansive worldview compared to my fellow cadets. That worldview shaped my actions and thoughts, and had brought me to this very situation. Plus, if I hadn't grown up with Salcombe, he might very well have tracked down the pieces of heart on his own. And without me trying to stop him, he could have succeeded in resurrecting the dragon god and destroying our world.

Even so, I couldn't let this go. I'd always wondered if I had relatives living somewhere in Elantia, people who would have wanted and loved me. If I did, if these people still existed and Salcombe had deprived me of them...

"You need to tell me about them," I said flatly, clamping down hard on my anger. "I deserve to know where I came from, and if I still have any living relatives." If I did, what did this mean for me? I was a member of House Tavarian, thanks to Lord Tavarian's sponsorship, but would that continue? Would he send me back to my family's house, if it still existed, or would he insist that I honor our agreement? Then again, would they even want me? There was so much I didn't know, and Salcombe had all the answers.

"You know where you came from," Salcombe said, just as flatly. "Your parentage doesn't change that. I will tell you that only one of your parents had dragon rider blood," he said before I could protest further. "But if you want to know the rest, you must help me finish my quest."

"What does that mean?" I demanded. "Help you find this piece, or all the others, too?"

"Who knows?" Salcombe smirked. "Maybe I'll tell you something about them every time we find a piece. A little incentive to keep you by my side."

I held back a snort at that. There was no way I was risking the fate of the world over the identity of my parents. But the tidbit Salcombe had given me niggled at the back of my mind. Only *one* of my parents had been a dragon rider. But which one? Had my father fallen in love with a commoner, or had it been the other way around? Was their love story similar to that of Rhia's ancestors? Her great-great-great-great-grandfather had married into an old dragon rider family, but because the family had never accepted them, the two had branched off and started their own, smaller house. Perhaps my parents had gone through a similar upheaval…

When we arrived home, I went straight up to my room, wanting to be alone with my thoughts. Unfortunately, a giant pile of boxes waited on my bed, preventing me from flopping onto it and burying my face in the pillows. Annoyed, I lifted the top off one of the boxes to see one of the dresses I'd ordered, a pale-yellow silk. My heart jolted, and I quickly sorted through the boxes, wondering if my court dress had arrived.

But the elaborate dress I'd ordered wasn't in the boxes, nor were the fancy hoops or ostrich feathers I would be forced to wear with them. I opened a round box to find one of the hats I'd ordered. It had a wide brim, meant to be worn slanted over my head. Not something I would have ever ordered on my own, but the pink silk roses and green leaves laden at the top would go very well with the garden dress the modiste had matched it with.

I was about to put the lid back on the box when my treasure sense flared to life. I usually kept it on low when I was in the house, since there were so many valuables here, but sometimes it had a mind of its own, activating when something important or magical was nearby. Curious, I lifted the hat from the box and found a small package nestled within, wrapped in brown paper. Tearing it open, I found one of the small, magical earpieces dragon riders used to communicate with each other over long distances.

*Could it be?* I thought, my heart pounding. Hastily, I fixed the earpiece to my right ear, then ducked into the bathing room for some privacy. *Please work, please work, please work,* I chanted silently as I pressed my fingertip to the small button on the outside of the device.

Long seconds passed as the device hummed in my ear. I was about to give up hope that someone would answer when the humming abruptly ceased. "Miss Kenrook?"

"Lord Tavarian!" I kept my voice to an excited whisper, even though I wanted to shout his name from the rooftops. Tears of joy and relief sprang to my eyes, and for the first time in weeks, I felt some of the weight slide off my shoulders. "Are you all right?"

"I'm still alive," Tavarian said, and the weariness in his voice made me pause. "What about you? Has Salcombe hurt you at all?"

"I'm fine," I said quickly. "But what's happened to you? You sound..." I didn't want to say "defeated," but that was the first thought that came to mind. "You aren't being kicked out of the country, are you?"

"Not yet," Tavarian said. "But someone attempted to assassinate me yet again, with a poisoned dart on my way back to my lodgings. I was able to get the antidote in time, but I am still recovering."

"Poison?" My heart kicked into a gallop as my stomach dropped, leaving me reeling. Here I was, bitching about having to go to court and play nice with snooty nobles, while Tavarian was dodging assassination attempts! "Dragon's balls! You shouldn't be going through this alone."

"I could say the same about you," he said, a hint of a smile in his voice. "But now that we have a way to communicate, we don't have to be quite so isolated anymore. Please don't worry about me, Zara," he added. "This is not the first time I have been at death's door, and it will not be the last."

He coaxed me into giving him an update, and I told him about the progress I'd made with Salcombe—or lack thereof—and about the upcoming court presentation we were to attend. I decided to leave out the bit about Salcombe knowing about my parentage—it wasn't relevant to our current circumstances, and Tavarian had enough to worry about without me throwing something new into the mix.

"I'm really worried about Lessie," I confided in him. "Every time I reach out to her through the bond, I sense anger. But she's too far away for us to communicate, so I have no idea what's going on."

"I know how you feel," Tavarian said. "Being separated from your dragon for long periods of time will naturally create a sense of anxiety within both of you. It took Muza and me a long time to find our...equilibrium. But so long as your dragon is not in physical pain, I would not assume the worst. If Lessie returned to the camp, she is probably being confined, in the absence of her rider, to prevent her from seeking you out."

"Chained up?" That would explain the anger. "But that's wrong! Lessie hasn't done anything to deserve being locked away."

"I know it seems wrong," Tavarian said, "but it is normal

procedure to do so with a dragon of Lessie's age. Partially-trained dragons are young and impetuous, and therefore very hard to control without their riders."

I sighed. "I guess so, but Lessie isn't going to see it that way. I hate the idea of her being locked up because of me. She might be a bit headstrong but she—" I cut myself off at the sound of someone knocking insistently on the door. "I have to go," I whispered.

"Please keep me updated," he said. He quickly gave me his address in case I needed to send word to him and couldn't get to the earpiece. "Take care, Miss Kenrook. Court is not for the faint of heart."

"Don't I know it," I muttered, disconnecting. I hid the earpiece in the cabinet beneath my bathroom sink, then went to answer the door, expecting the maid.

Instead, it was Trolbos who filled the doorway with his menacing bulk. "What do you want?" I cried, instinctively reaching for my absent daggers.

Trolbos ignored me. "Who were you talking to?" he barked, backing me into a corner. His black eyes blazed with fury, his teeth bared in a snarl.

"I wasn't talking to anyone!" My heart pounded erratically against my breast as he pressed a hand against the base of my throat, not quite choking me. "Let me go!"

"Don't lie to me! I heard your voice as I passed your door." His grip on my throat tightened, fingers digging in hard enough to bruise. "Tell me the truth!"

I tried to speak, but a strangled gasp was all that came out. My vision was already starting to swim from lack of oxygen, panic a living, breathing thing in my chest. Trolbos's massive body pressed against mine, close enough that I could feel the press of his many knives. I snatched one from its sheath on pure instinct and stabbed his heart, only for the strike to reverberate through my wrist as it bounced back against something.

Trolbos laughed, a dark, delighted sound that made my blood freeze. "Think I wouldn't take precautions, bitch? I wear chain mail under my clothes at all times." He knocked the knife from my hand, and it clattered to the floor as he crushed my body against the wall again, leaving me no room to make another grab for his weapons.

"I'm not going to ask you again." His rancid breath was hot against my skin, and this time I felt more than just his knives pressing against me. "Tell me who you were talking to."

"Trolbos!" The door banged open and Salcombe strode in, his eyes wide with anger. "What are you doing!"

Trolbos didn't budge. "I heard her talking to someone in here," he growled, not even looking at Salcombe. Frustration warred with bloodlust, and I could tell he was furious at being interrupted. "If you'd give me a minute, I'll get the bitch to tell us who."

"Let her go at once!" Salcombe snapped. When Trolbos still didn't move, Salcombe took a step forward. The atmosphere in the room changed at once, and I sensed something dark and ominous swirling in the air around Salcombe. *"Do I need to repeat myself?"*

The fury in Trolbos's eyes wavered, replaced by a flicker of fear. "No, master," he said respectfully, finally withdrawing from me.

I nearly collapsed to the floor in relief. "Thank you," I said tightly, wrapping my arms around myself to hide the fact that I was trembling like a leaf.

Salcombe made no move to approach me, his gaze flicking to the knife on the ground. "Who drew that?" he demanded.

"I did, when that brute of yours started choking me." I glared at Trolbos. "He heard me mumbling to myself and charged in here like a wild animal. He probably would have raped me if you hadn't barged in!"

"That's a filthy lie," Trolbos spat. But lust still lurked behind that angry gaze. "Why would I want you? You're nothing but gutter trash."

"That is *enough*." Salcombe jabbed a finger at the door. "Get out."

Trolbos stiffened. "But—"

"*Now!*"

He shot me one last glare, then stalked out of the room. I grimaced as he slammed the door behind him, hard enough to rattle the hinges.

Salcombe sighed, weariness settling into his face. Suddenly he looked every bit his age, despite the disguise he wore. "I will punish him appropriately," he told me, the closest I'd get to an apology. "This won't happen again."

"How can you promise that, when we still live in the same house?" I countered. "It's obvious Trolbos has had it in for me since day one. You should give me back one of my weapons, in case he barges in here aga—"

"I *said* that it won't happen again," Salcombe interrupted. His lip curled in disgust as he took in the bruises on my neck and my rumpled dress. "Get yourself cleaned up before Lady Astilla arrives," he ordered. "I don't want her thinking that I beat you."

*That wouldn't be far from the truth,* I almost said as he strode out. But I sighed, then rang for my maid so she could help me hide the evidence of Trolbos's abuse. I was going to have to be more careful the next time I contacted Tavarian. I might have convinced Salcombe that Trolbos was hearing things this time, but I knew better than to think luck struck twice.

FIVE

"I can't believe that I spent a whole week prepping just so I could spend hours standing around," I grumbled to Salcombe as we waited in line outside the great hall in the palace, surrounded by a crush of other nobles. I imagined we wouldn't take up nearly as much space if we weren't forced to wear these ridiculously wide hoops, but perhaps it was for the best.

"This is the game we play," Salcombe said mildly. He was standing to my right, dressed in long coattails and pantaloons, as was the custom for men being presented at court. The silver wig perched atop his head looked especially ridiculous, but the humor I'd found in it had long worn off after we had been forced to wait in the carriage for several hours, just so that we could spend *more* hours waiting to be admitted to the great hall. "Be thankful that you are here as a married woman and not a debutante. At least your future does not hinge on this moment."

*No, just my life,* I thought sarcastically. But I knew what he meant. Most of the women in line around me were much younger, anywhere from sixteen to eighteen, their slim forms rigidly straight despite the crushing weight of the jewelry and silks they wore. These women were being presented to the court for the very first time—a "coming out" that marked their "official entry into womanhood and the marriage mart," Lady Astilla had explained to me. Normally, these women would have been presented to the queen, but the queen was no longer in residence at the palace. Apparently, she had recently been banished to some northern island, and had been dragged kicking and screaming from the palace by the royal guard. So the king was presiding over the presentations for the debutantes along with the other court presentations, and naturally that was causing quite a bit of consternation.

"It's preposterous," Lady Astilla had said as she oversaw my preparations this morning. The dress had arrived, exactly as I'd envisioned it, and I would have looked amazing if I hadn't also been draped in ostrich feathers and heavy emeralds. Even so, I did get quite a few envious looks from the debutantes, who were forced to wear either white or very light colors, as I'd alighted from the carriage. "It would be one thing if our king was a dignified man, but instead he is going to slobber all over those poor girls while Lady Hariana wiggles around in his lap. No debutante should have to endure such indignities during one of the most important ceremonies of her life!"

I'd had to stop from rolling my eyes. I'd been shot at, punched, stabbed, jailed, and kidnapped multiple times in my life. If the worst these women ever had to suffer was the king leering at their bosoms and making some lewd remarks, they led very privileged lives indeed.

*That isn't quite fair,* I chided myself. After all, many of these women were forced into arranged marriages by their families, sometimes to men twice their age. A wealthy life was not necessarily a happy life.

Eventually, Salcombe and I made it to the doors of the great hall. The guards checked both of us for weapons before allowing us to pass through the double doors and into the grand space where the king's courtiers mingled. They lounged on couches and chairs grouped on either side of the hall, nursing glasses of wine or picking at small plates of cheese as they gossiped or talked business. Many of them looked over the ladies with interest, and I felt quite a few gazes pause on me and Salcombe, taking in my vibrant peacock dress and red hair. I had to fight the urge not to stare longingly at them—those couches looked quite comfortable, especially with my feet hurting in these heels.

"There," Salcombe murmured in my ear, startling me. We hadn't spoken in nearly an hour. "Playing chess by the hearth. That's the man we need to speak to."

Discreetly, I looked where Salcombe had indicated. A man with chin-length black hair and a red velvet hat was sitting at a walnut table, playing chess with a balding man. He stroked his goatee as he considered the board, his attention wholly focused on the game. My chest tightened, unsure how to feel about his presence—if Salcombe did get what he wanted from the man, that meant we would be leaving soon. And I would be separated from Lord Tavarian yet again.

*You're just going to have to figure out how to get the heart away from Salcombe if we find it,* I told myself firmly. If I could get hold of another piece of heart, that would put two out of Salcombe's immediate reach. I knew better than to think that the tentative peace between Salcombe and me could last forever; eventually, he would want me to help him retrieve Tavarian's piece of heart from wherever he'd hidden it, and if I refused, he would try to use me as a bargaining chip. The dragon god-inflicted madness Salcombe suffered from may have been temporarily absent, but it would return with a vengeance the moment I tried to interfere with his goals.

"We're here," Salcombe muttered, jolting me from my reverie. "Be ready."

I sucked in a breath. We stood right outside the doors to the presence chamber—the king's inner sanctum, where he gathered with his most trusted courtiers. Steeling myself, we stepped through the open double doors together, my hand on Salcombe's arm.

The presence chamber was significantly smaller than the great hall, but still large—my entire apartment could fit in this space, I thought as we began the slow walk toward the dais at the end of the room. Nearly two dozen pairs of eyes fixed on me as we approached, but I ignored them all, focusing on the king. He was an extraordinarily fat man, his bejeweled clothing straining at the buttons to contain his bulk, with a ruddy face and thinning blond hair mostly hidden by his crown. His thick blond beard helped hide some of the fat rolls around his jawline, and I could tell if I looked closely enough that he had once been a handsome man, but there was no getting around it—King Zoltar had really let himself go.

And yet, even with the slovenly state of his body, the king still had an air of command around him. His bulk was intimidating, and he sat straight in his chair, making the most of his broad shoulders. I might have even taken him seriously, if not for the fact that a young woman was draped across his lap, her slender arm looped around his neck. She wore a dress of pale gold that clung to her curvy figure, and an absolutely garish necklace and tiara encrusted in rubies that matched the brooch the king wore. My treasure sense told me they were incredibly valuable, and I had a feeling they were part of the Traggaran crown jewels. As she leaned forward a little, scrutinizing us with eyes of dark chocolate, I half-expected her breasts to tumble right out of her bodice.

But the king barely paid her any mind. His eyes were on me as Salcombe and I were announced, and as I sank into the awkward curtsy I'd spent hours practicing, I could feel his gaze glued to *my* breasts peeking out from behind the peacock feathers. Lady Astilla had thwarted my attempts at modesty by forcing the maid to cinch my corset as tight as it would possibly go, forcing my breasts in and up. Apparently, just because she didn't approve of the king's lascivious behavior didn't mean she wasn't going to help him feast his eyes on my chest.

"You may rise," the king finally said.

Salcombe and I did so. "You have a very lovely wife, Lord

Trentiano," the king said to Salcombe, though his eyes were still on me. "Have the two of you been married long?"

"Two years," Salcombe said smoothly. He settled a hand on my waist, and even though I found these necessary public displays of affection repulsive, I appreciated the act more than ever under the scrutiny of the king's gaze. Judging by the glint in his eye, I had a feeling that if Hariana wasn't in his lap, he would have invited me to come and take her spot, husband be damned.

Hariana seemed to know it too, for she twined herself more tightly around the king. "My king, surely we should move these people along," she purred, thrusting her well-endowed chest into his face. "There is still a long line of people waiting, and I want to get through them quickly so we can enjoy a bit of time together before the garden party."

The way she wriggled in his lap told me *exactly* how she planned to spend that time, and I had to hide a grimace of disgust as the king gave her a piggish grin of delight. "Very well," he said, waving a meaty hand toward us. His other hand crept up Lady Hariana's skirts, and she gave a girlish giggle in response. "You may pass on."

The ripple through the observing crowd told me that the courtiers did *not* approve of Zoltar's scandalous behavior. Salcombe and I bowed and curtsied one more time before slowly backing out of the room—Lady Astilla taught me it was considered extremely rude to turn your back on royalty. As the king buried his face in Lady Hariana's chest, Salcombe caught my eye. I nearly lost my composure at the look of incredulity and disgust in his eyes, and had to bury a swell of sudden laughter at the absurdity of the situation.

"What a pathetic man," Salcombe said under his breath, once we were *far* out of earshot of both the king and his courtiers. "Another idiot who rules by his loins instead of his brain. It is a wonder he manages to get anything done with that floozy squirming in his lap."

"At least you don't need anything from him," I said, although part of me wished that he did. If I could gain access to the king's ear, perhaps I had a shot at changing his mind about allying with Zallabar.

*Yeah, right,* I thought as I remembered the way he groped Lady Hariana in front of all those men. Who was I kidding? Women were nothing but playthings to a man like Zoltar. The only thing he'd want from me was my body, and I'd sooner stab my own eyes out than debase myself like that.

Salcombe steered us toward the chess table where the man he'd wanted to speak to had been, but two different players occupied the board, and he was nowhere to be found. We spent the next two hours hanging around, mingling with the other courtiers while we waited for the servants to finish preparing the royal gardens for the reception.

"That dress looks like something from last century," a woman dripping in pink silk and lace said as she looked me up and down with a critical eye. "Did you find it in a consignment shop? I can't imagine any modiste worth her salt would have made something so out of fashion."

The real Zara would have thrown back some snarky retort, but since I was *Lady* Zara, I merely smiled. "If I did, perhaps it was at the same shop you frequent," I said, giving her diamond necklace a pointed look. My treasure sense told me that they were fakes, worth less than a quarter of what a real diamond necklace would go for. Her family had likely fallen on hard times and she'd sold the real necklace to pay off some debts.

"I have no idea what you're talking about," the woman said, but her face went sheet-white, and she unconsciously lifted a slender hand to her faux necklace. I hid a smirk as she struggled to change the subject, knowing she was likely terrified that I would expose her for the fraud she was. "A lady of my stature would have no need to patronize such a shop!"

Lady Zara: one. Stuffy Nobles: zero.

Thankfully, the steward came in and announced the garden was now open to guests, giving the woman an out. The side doors to the great hall had been thrown wide, and the crowd of bored nobles immediately spilled out, heading for the expansive gardens. Salcombe and I made a few more rounds before he ended up in a spirited conversation with a man who turned out to be the royal librarian. The conversation was actually fascinating, but after a few moments, Salcombe strongly hinted at me to make myself scarce. I tried not to be insulted as I did as I was told and wandered off—I knew it was easier for Salcombe to extract information out of these highbrows when I *wasn't* around, as men tended not to speak freely in front of the gentler sex.

Annoyed, I grabbed a glass of wine from a passing server and nursed it as I floated through the crowd. In no mood to indulge the various inane conversations swirling around me, I eavesdropped on a group of naval officers sitting on a trio of benches that curved around a fountain sculpture of a mermaid.

Her bared breasts would have been shocking enough, but the streams of water spurting from her nipples were an attraction in their own right. I wondered if King Zoltar had installed the piece himself, or if it had been commissioned by a former king. The idea that all Traggaran kings were as piggish as the current monarch made me glad to have been born in Elantia, not here. Yes, there were problems with our republic, but at least we didn't have to deal with men like *this*.

"Quite a party, isn't it?" one of the officers said as he raised his glass to the others. "One of the last we'll be enjoying for a while, I think."

"Thank gods for that," another man said heartily. "We've been waiting nearly two months for the king to sign that declaration of war, cooling our heels on the shores when we should be sticking our swords in Elantian bellies."

"You mean sticking our cocks into Elantian whores," another officer said.

My stomach curdled as the officers laughed. "We'll be doing both soon enough," another man said. "The king is going to sign the declaration tomorrow, and the general will give us our orders that same afternoon. The armada is nearly ready to go and will be finished in time for the new cannons to arrive. Those dragon-riding bastards won't know what hit them!"

Not wanting to hear more, I moved away from the officers. As I passed into another clearing, I saw the king had finally emerged from his chambers and was mingling with the nobles. He roared with laughter at something one of his courtiers said, jowls quivering, and Lady Hariana simpered as she leaned into him, trying to wrest his attention back to her. I curled my lip as I watched his big hand slide down her back to splay against the curve of her ass. A wave of disgust filled me, and suddenly I wished I had my knives. It would be so easy to bury a dagger in the king's back, to end his miserable life and my woes all at once. If the king was dead, he couldn't sign the declaration, could he?

But no, I thought, depression settling into my bones. That wouldn't work. I was no assassin, and even if I could kill the king in cold blood, that wouldn't help us. The king's death might delay the war for a few days, but I would likely be hanged as an Elantian spy, and the new king would have even more reason to go to war with my country. Words, not weapons, were the only thing that could sway Zoltar from his path, and the only person who could wield those words effectively was nowhere to be found at the party tonight.

Thoroughly fed up with watching the king, I wandered off, looking for Salcombe. Had he found Elliot yet? Perhaps I could sneak up on the two of them together and do some eavesdropping. When Salcombe relayed these conversations to me, he only told me what he deemed salient, which meant I could be missing out on vital clues.

Lost in thought, I rounded a corner, and nearly ran straight into someone. "Lady Zara!" Firm hands gripped my shoulders. "Are you all right?"

"General Trattner!" My cheeks colored, and I hastily stepped back. "I'm so sorry. I didn't look where I was going."

"No need to apologize," he said kindly. "There's no harm done. But are you sure you're all right? You look as if something has upset you."

"Oh, it's nothing," I lied. "I merely wish I was home, so I could get out of this silly dress. Court garments are quite cumbersome."

"Indeed." He gave me a sympathetic look. "I can't imagine having to wear all the fussy contraptions you females put up with on the regular. I think I would die if I had to wear a corset all day. Whoever said women are the weaker sex is a fool."

I laughed and took his offered arm. The two of us fell into easy conversation, as we always did, talking of Zallabar. But this time, the general seemed more interested in talking about his career as a soldier than the ancient history we usually discussed.

"I confess I miss the old days, back when I was a soldier and only had to worry about following orders and carrying out the tasks I was given," Trattner said morosely. "The weight of command is difficult enough, but now that I am a diplomat as well, I must be careful to watch my tongue at all times."

"I can sympathize with that," I said, and I meant that more than he could ever know. During my all-too-brief stint in the military I felt I couldn't be honest with anyone, and I hadn't even been a diplomat! I couldn't imagine how men like Trattner and Tavarian felt, having to constantly put on a show for others and hide their real feelings and opinions. "It must be especially difficult when you have to deal with heads of state."

"It is...trying," Trattner said, seeming to struggle with himself. I could tell part of him wanted to confide more, but his sense of duty and self-preservation were holding him back. "But never mind that, Lady Zara. I don't wish to bore you with my quibbles. Overall, life is quite good, and things are moving in the right direction."

We turned a corner and found ourselves right outside a tall hedge that seemed to stretch for quite a distance.

"What is this?" I asked, placing a hand against the thick wall of vegetation.

"The royal hedge maze." A breathy moan floated across the air toward us from the other side of the hedge, and General Trattner's eyes flashed with distaste as he lowered his voice. "The unwary visitor can get quite lost in there, but for the natives, it is a favorite place for dalliances, as there are many private nooks and benches within. I would not suggest attempting to traverse it during gatherings such as this one, unless you'd like to come across a rather unpleasant surprise."

I laughed at the look of utter disgust on his face. "It sounds like you are speaking from experience," I said as we walked along the outside of the maze.

He shuddered. "A tale I would rather not speak of."

My treasure sense pinged, and I paused as another breathy moan floated up from beyond the hedge. Both seemed to be coming from a spot several yards ahead, and as I focused, I realized that they were the crown jewels Lady Hariana and the king had been wearing earlier. The two of them must be in the maze, engaging in that "private time" Hariana had promised the king right in front of Salcombe and me. My initial instinct was to steer Trattner away from the area—I had no desire to hear more—but just as I was about to, an idea struck me.

A brilliant, terrible idea.

"General," I said as we continued to walk, "would you tell me about your family? You seem very fond of them, and I would have you talk of something that lifts your spirits, especially on a lovely night like this. How did you and your wife meet?"

The general immediately lit up. "It's quite a funny tale," he began.

As he talked, I surreptitiously passed my hand over the sparkling glass of wine the general held and pressed the button on the side of the ring that Salcombe had given me. The general didn't notice the two drops of serum that fell into his wine glass, and when I lifted my own glass to my lips, he automatically followed suit. By this time, we'd passed the spot where the king and Lady Hariana were necking, so we walked to the other end of the maze, then turned around and headed back.

As we neared the spot where the king and his mistress were hidden, I suddenly bent over, clutching my foot. "Oooh," I moaned in pain, switching from Zallabarian to Traggaran to make sure we were overheard. "I hate these slippers so much! I think I have a blister forming."

"Do you need to sit down?" Trattner asked, automatically switching languages as well. He likely would have questioned the change had he been in his right mind, but the serum was in his blood now, affecting his judgment. He immediately steered me over to a nearby bench, which was exactly my intention. "Here, let me see that foot."

"Oh no, I couldn't," I demurred, tucking my legs beneath my skirts. "Someone might come upon us. It would be very improper for you to be examining my foot."

"To hell with propriety," Trattner grumbled—more proof that the serum had taken effect. "I have basic medical training from my days on the battlefield, and always carry a few supplies with me. I see no reason why you should suffer needlessly." But he didn't push the matter, and a pang of guilt hit me. General Trattner was a genuinely good man...did I really want to do this to him?

*He may be a good man, but he's still the enemy.*

"General," I said, steering his attention before he started to push the matter again—I did, in fact, have a blister on my big toe, but that wasn't the point—"how does a man of your distinction feel about King Zoltar's court, and the Traggarans in general? From the few times you have mentioned them, you don't seem entirely impressed."

Trattner's nostrils flared, his eyes too bright. "That is because there is nothing to be impressed about," he said bluntly, fully under the drug's influence now. "The people here are lazy and dishonest, and the soldiers are preening amateurs, barely fit for battle. If not for Traggar's fairly impressive navy, we wouldn't give a thought to allying with them."

"Really?" I pressed a hand to my breast, as if shocked. "But Traggar has won quite a few wars. They have many colonies in the south, don't they?"

"Yes, and again, that is thanks to their navy. The king certainly knows how to use it, and again, that is the primary reason we are allying with him. But our own ruler has never had any love for Zoltar, and now that I have met the man myself, I can see why. He is a fat, ugly fool,

led by his privates and has lost all sense of responsibility. I heard all about how he fondled that trollop of his, draped in the crown jewels, in front of all those innocent young ladies presenting themselves today—such poor taste would never be tolerated in Zallabar."

*"How dare you!"*

The general froze as King Zoltar stormed from behind the hedge maze, adjusting his pantaloons along the way. His face was beet-red with fury, and he jabbed a meaty finger at Trattner. "You have spent the last several weeks at my court, enjoying my hospitality and everything I have to offer, and you think you can speak of me this way, in my own garden! I'll have you sent back to Zallabar in pieces, you ungrateful worm!"

"Your Majesty." Trattner rose from the bench, his face marble-white. "I did not mean—"

"He meant every word," Lady Hariana said, clutching the king's arm. She was just as furious, the color in her cheeks high, her dark eyes sparkling with rage. "I told you there was something off about him, Your Highness. The Zallabarians have never considered Traggar to be an equal—they think of us as uncouth heathens, even as they sit on our doorstep begging for our help! What kind of allies are these?"

Murmurs of agreement rippled through the crowd that had gathered around. Despite Lady Hariana's disheveled appearance—her corset laces were undone and one of her breasts was dangerously close to tumbling out of her dress—all eyes were on General Trattner, who looked like he would prefer to do nothing more than sink into the ground and never come back up again. Another wave of guilt hit me, and I put my hand on his arm instinctively, wanting to comfort him. An absurd urge, since I was the one who'd put him in this predicament, but I couldn't help it.

The king's eyes bulged as he noticed the motion.

"Get out!" he bellowed. "*Both* of you!"

"Your Majesty—"

"You are no longer permitted to address me, General Trattner," the king spat as guards converged on the both of us. "You are banished from my court, and ordered to leave my country *post-haste*. Be sure to tell Richstein he can take his alliance and shove it up his bony arse when you return home to inform him of your failure!"

"Your Majesty." Salcombe elbowed his way to my side and seized my arm. "Is my wife in some sort of trouble?"

The king turned his bugged-out gaze on Salcombe. "You and your wife are no longer welcome at court either," he spat. "I saw how the chit sympathized with this witless worm after he insulted my country. Begone, both of you, before I have her jailed!"

The royal guards promptly escorted us from the premises, shocked murmurs following us all the way to the gates. Salcombe said nothing, and I glanced at him curiously out of the corner of my eye. I expected him to be angry about this, but he seemed remarkably calm, unfazed by the wave of gossip and scandal I'd created. My gut was a mass of roiling emotions—elation, fear, guilt. There was no way King Zoltar would sign that declaration of war now, even if the Zallabarian government sent him an entire harem of women to make up for their ambassador's grave insult.

Traggar was well and truly out of the picture.

"That was very clever, Zara," he said once we were alone together in the carriage.

I blinked, the picture of innocence. "I have no idea what you're talking about."

"It doesn't require genius to deduce that you coaxed the general into confessing his true feelings about Traggar within earshot of the king." His gaze dropped to the ring on my finger. "That is not what I had intended you to use the serum for, but I suppose I cannot fault you for wanting to protect our country. I now understand why you were so keen on getting close to General Trattner. Was this Lord Tavarian's idea?"

My insides froze, but I managed to hold onto my composure. "Tavarian and I haven't spoken since the garden party," I said. "But I imagine that he will be quite happy when he learns of this development. Perhaps Zoltar will finally invite him to court."

"Hmph." Salcombe's eyes narrowed with suspicion, but he did not press the matter. "You may have found a way to help your knight in shining armor, but he will not be able to save you, Zara. We are leaving for Lord Fanuel's estate tomorrow."

My spine stiffened. "Tomorrow? So you've managed to ferret out the location, then?"

Salcombe smirked. "I did quite a bit more than that. Lord Rycroft has agreed to give me a letter of introduction to take with me. Lord Fanuel has taken up residence in a small seaside village to the south. If we leave early tomorrow, we should arrive the following afternoon. It is quite fortunate in a way that you got us ejected from the party, as that gives us more time to prepare for our departure."

"Great," I said, hiding a grimace at the irony. It was considered extremely rude to retire before the king, so if not for the scandal I'd created with Trattner, we'd likely have been stuck at that party until the wee hours of the morning.

The carriage ride back to the townhouse seemed to drag on forever, and by the time we pulled up in front of the temporary residence, it took everything in me not to fling myself out of the conveyance and race up the stairs to my room. As it was, it took nearly an hour before I was allowed any sort of privacy—the maid had to get me out of my court dress and all the contraptions that went with it, plus stow all the jewels and remove the hundreds of pins in my hair.

"Do you need anything el—"

"Just some peace and quiet, please," I interrupted. "I have had a very trying day. Thank you for your help," I added, not wanting to be too rude.

The maid quickly made herself scarce, and I let out a sigh of relief. I hadn't been joking about the need for peace and quiet—my head was pounding, my feet aching, and a big part of me wanted nothing more than to flop onto the bed and close my eyes.

Instead, I grabbed the magical earpiece from its hiding place and headed straight for the bathroom.

"Miss Kenrook?" Tavarian's voice came through on the third try. "Is everything all right?"

"More than all right," I assured him. "You should try to get another invite to court tomorrow. I have a feeling the king is going to be more than willing to see you now."

There was a long pause. "What did you do, Zara?"

I grinned, then launched into the tale. Now that the ordeal was behind me, the enormity of what I'd done was finally sinking in. Yes, I felt bad for throwing General Trat-tner to the wolves, but only because I liked him as an individ-ual. He might like me too, but if he'd ever found out that I was Elantian military, he would have me thrown into the dungeons without hesitation. He was here to destroy my coun-try, and if humiliating him in front of the king had been what it took to save my people, I would do it again a thousand times over.

"This is incredible," Tavarian said when I'd finished. He sounded a bit dazed, as if he were recovering from a hard hit to the head. "I was about to pen a letter to the council to tell them that the declaration was being signed tomorrow, and that we should prepare to be hit on two fronts. But because of your inge-nuity, everything has changed. You've achieved the impossible, Zara. I can't thank you enough for what you've done."

To my surprise, emotion welled in my chest. Had anyone ever sounded so proud of me before? "You don't have to thank me," I said, struggling against the sudden lump in my throat. "You've done so much for me and Lessie, Tavarian. And this isn't only about helping you out. This situation affects the fate of our entire country."

"I know that better than almost anyone," he said roughly. "And that makes me appreciate it all the more. The moment I am done with the king, the two of us will return home, and I will have you acquitted of whatever trumped-up charges the military court has decided to pin on you. As far as I am concerned, you are a war hero, and what you have done today should be more than enough to get you and Lessie excused from the front lines so that you can resume your training in safety."

This time, the tears really *did* fall from my cheeks. "That might be easier said than done," I said shakily.

"Why?" Tavarian's tone changed as he sensed my anguish. "What's wrong, Zara?"

*Zara.* Were we on a first-name basis, now? Should I start calling him Varrick? But no, that didn't seem right. "Salcombe found out the location of the mage he's been looking for," I said heavily. "We're leaving tomorrow morning."

"Do you know where?"

"Some seaside village to the south." I pressed my head against the wall, exhaustion seeping into my bones. I was so close to being reunited with Lessie again, and yet so far away. "He didn't say which one."

"Blast it." Tavarian was silent for a long moment. "I could come and get you now."

"No." I shook my head, even though he couldn't see. "You need to take advantage of the opportunity and secure an alliance with Zoltar before someone reminds him of his hatred for Elantians. Salcombe might be on the outs with the king right now, but he hasn't been outright banished from Traggar, and he still has plenty of friends. If you try to take me from him, he might find a way to get you kicked out before you can see the king."

"You're right," Tavarian said, resigned. "The king must be dealt with. I am glad the spectacle you created was so public—it will be easy for me to ensure that the exact nature of the argument is spread far and wide, to eliminate any chance of the king forgiving Zallabar for their slight against him. I will be paying visits to the gutter presses right away. If everything goes well, I should wrap things up in a few days. Truthfully, it is best that you leave the capital now anyway—the factions who were trying to block me from seeing Zoltar will be furious at having a profitable war snatched from them at the last moment, and if they find out you are the reason they will come after you. But the magical earpieces won't function once you leave the city, Zara. It's quite possible I won't be able to reconnect with you again."

"It's okay," I said, though I felt anything but. "Heading south should put me closer to the channel." And thus, the military camp. "I might be able to reach Lessie at that distance."

"She will have a difficult time coming to you, as she'll be under guard," Tavarian warned. "If she is unable to get away, I will head to the camp myself once I have completed my business here and try to secure her release myself."

"Thank you," I said fervently. Even if Lessie wasn't able to come get me, knowing that Tavarian would check on her once he was done here took a weight off my shoulders. I hated knowing she was suffering in captivity day after day and there was nothing I could do about it.

"No, thank *you*," Tavarian said. "I mean it, Zara—you are a hero. Your actions tonight have saved countless lives. No matter what anyone else might say to you, I will always remember what you have done."

I laughed through my tears. "Now you're laying it on thick."

"Don't be silly," Tavarian said. "The only people I go out of my way to flatter are despot kings and warmongering emperors."

That startled a laugh out of me. "And ground-dwelling thieves, apparently."

I could hear the smile in his voice. "You are far more than

that, and you know it. Don't give up hope, Zara. I know it may not feel like it, but you are not alone."

I held those words close to me as I retired for the night. I might not have managed to derail Salcombe yet, but things were finally going in the right direction. *Something* had to give soon. It was just a matter of when.

SIX

As planned, Salcombe and I set off bright and early for Lord Fanuel's estate. As the carriage rolled along the paved roads, heading out of the capital, I turned my attention to the golden dawn rising outside the window and did my best to ignore the shivers that crawled up my spine at Trolbos's proximity. My brief reprieve from him was long past—Salcombe wasn't going to leave his right-hand man behind even if he had tried to strangle and rape me. But between Trolbos and the second guard, who sat right next to me, it was almost claustrophobic in the carriage.

*Stay positive,* I told myself, breathing deeply. I may not have figured out how to thwart Salcombe yet, but I'd figure out a way. After all, I'd just managed to foil the plans of an entire nation, hadn't I? Surely I could do the same with a single man, even if he was far better versed in the art of manipulation than I was.

"What are you smiling about?" Trolbos grunted. He glared

at me and seemed surlier than ever. I was pretty sure he hated that Salcombe had forced him to back off these past few days and thought that I was given entirely too much leeway. "Think you've figured out a way to escape?"

I smiled sweetly—my version of flipping him the bird. "I'm just enjoying the ride," I said. "The city has been interesting, but it'll be nice to see some of the countryside, don't you think?"

Trolbos grunted.

"I think you will enjoy Whitmouth quite a bit," Salcombe said. "By all accounts, it is a picturesque village with lovely beaches. Not my cup of tea—I much prefer the mountains. But I remember how much you enjoyed the sea whenever I took you to a coastal town as a child. You thought starfish were the most fascinating creatures," he said fondly.

I blinked—Salcombe rarely brought up my childhood memories. "I still do think they're fascinating," I said, a smile tugging at my lips. "Did you know that they can regenerate if you cut off their limbs? It takes up to a year, but that's still pretty impressive. I can't even regrow my pinky toe."

Trolbos glowered, thoroughly unimpressed. He hated these little bonding moments Salcombe and I shared, and rightfully so. The more Salcombe saw me as his foster child, the more he let his guard down. I was more than happy to play right into that hand, with the hopes that I'd either be able to eventually get through to him or find a way to slip the noose before he could tighten it.

*I need to figure out a way to get my weapons back,* I thought. They were somewhere in the luggage—I could feel them calling to me through my treasure sense, the absence of them nearly as keen as Lessie's. Trolbos would be a lot less intimidating if I had my dragon blade in hand again. Maybe I could rummage through the luggage when we stopped for the night, under the pretense of looking for my nightgown or something.

But when we did stop for the night at a cozy rural inn, there was no opportunity. Salcombe's thugs slept in an adjoining room with the luggage, and since they handed over the single bag that held my basic belongings, I had no excuse to go through the rest of our things. Annoyed, I was forced to retire to the room Salcombe and I shared as husband and wife, tossing and turning on the couch while he snored away on the bed. Now that we were away from court, Salcombe's sense of chivalry was gone—after all, he was an old man, far past his couch sleeping days, and there was no way in hell we were sharing the bed.

We continued on our journey the next day, with Salcombe well rested. He seemed a bit haggard over the last few days, but there was a flush in his cheeks and a brightness in his eyes that suggested he'd snuck a bit more of that dragon god elixir. Reaching out with my treasure sense—the elixir was very valuable, easily detected—I noticed that he had far less than when he'd first kidnapped me from Tavarian's hidden valley estate. Perhaps he was forced to ration it. How long did a dosage last?

It was close to noon before we finally arrived at our destination. "Look," Salcombe said, pointing out the window. Tall cliffs loomed over a charming village from one side, and the sparkling sea lapped its shore from the other. "Lord Fanuel's estate is at the top."

I looked closer at the cliffs, and indeed, there was an estate perched at the edge, overlooking the channel. I wondered if I would be able to see Elantia's shores from up there, and a wave of homesickness almost overwhelmed me. Reaching through the bond, I tried to contact Lessie. Frustration simmered in my blood as I called her name again and again, to no avail. The strong sense of discontent was still prevalent in the bond, but there was no answer. Was she still too far away or merely asleep?

Circumventing the town, the carriage took the winding road up to the top of the cliffs. In no time at all, we pulled up to the gates of Lord Fanuel's estate. We were stopped by the guards, but the driver presented the letter of introduction from Fanuel's cousin, and they let us through.

"Wow," I murmured as the carriage rumbled up the paved road. The estate was at least ten acres of green fields and orchards, with a large mansion built on the far end, close enough to the cliff edge to provide spectacular views while far enough that the property wouldn't tumble into the ocean in the event of a landslide. The mansion was all white stone and terra-cotta roof tile, its wide arches and expansive windows lending an air of welcome. My treasure sense came to life as we stopped in front of the main entrance, and my blood thrummed as all sorts of valuables called to me.

Salcombe immediately noticed my excitement. "Do you sense the heart?" he demanded.

I shook my head. "No. But Lord Fanuel has quite a collection of magical artifacts. You should ask to see them."

To my surprise, Salcombe shook his head. "I do not wish to

waste time," he said. "We are here for one purpose. Do not allow yourself to become distracted, Zara."

The henchman sitting next to me opened the carriage door, then helped me down. As I waited for Trolbos and Salcombe to follow, I soaked in the atmosphere. The faint sound of the waves crashing below blended seamlessly with the sound of gulls cawing, and the gentle breeze teased my skin, bringing the scent of the ocean with it. I had a sudden urge to rush around to the other side of the mansion so I could go to the edge of the cliff and look out at the view.

Instead, I took Salcombe's arm, and we walked up the stairs and to the front entrance.

A butler opened the door before we could knock. "Good afternoon, Lord and Lady Trentiano," he said. "Please, come in."

"Thank you." Salcombe sounded pleased as we stepped into the foyer. A large bowl of fresh flowers dominated the table in the center of the room, and sunlight shimmered in through the skylight set in the arched ceiling overhead, opening up the space and lending a freshness to the cream-colored walls and smooth birch floorboards. "Lord Fanuel is aware of our arrival?"

"Indeed, and he invites you to luncheon with him on the terrace."

The butler led us through the home, which was simultaneously grand and welcoming, very much like the foyer. The same cream-colored walls, high ceilings, and birch floors followed us, but there were more masculine touches in the mahogany furniture and dark wood beams set into the ceilings. Each room we passed boasted wide windows offering amazing views of the ocean, framed by white or pale blue curtains. More than once, I was tempted to go through one of the open doors and explore, but since we hadn't been invited to do so, I forced myself to follow Salcombe and the butler.

As we stepped through the double doors and onto the terrace, my mood lifted considerably. The space was absolutely beautiful, shaded by a rose-covered trellis, and offered an expansive view of the ocean. The sky was remarkably clear, offering an unobstructed view of the Elantian coast. A pang of envy and sadness hit me, and I wished Lessie were here. I tried to reach out to her again, but still received no answer.

"My lord," the butler said as a man rose from a table that had already been set for three. He was middle-aged, with salt-and-pepper hair, and wore a set of pale blue robes—unusual dress for Traggaran nobles, who favored breeches and doublets. "Lord and Lady Trentiano are here."

"So they are." Lord Fanuel smiled politely as he extended a hand to Salcombe. His eyes were pale, somewhere between blue and gray, yet sharp as a blade as he studied us. "My cousin Elliot tells me that you are a magical scholar of sorts."

"A historian," Salcombe corrected smoothly, shaking the man's hand. "Ancient history and magical history often overlap, as I'm sure you already know. My wife, Zara," he added.

"Charmed." Fanuel took my hand, briefly pressing his lips against my skin, and from the way his eyes warmed, I could tell he meant it. "Please, sit and eat while you tell me what it is you're seeking. I can't promise that I will be helpful, but if it is magical history you are looking into, I am the most qualified expert in the country."

We sat down at the table and tucked into the simple but excellently cooked seafood meal, paired with glasses of sparkling wine. Again, I was struck by the sheer loveliness of the atmosphere. The high cliffs would make it a perfect home for Lessie and me, and I wondered if a similar property could be purchased in Elantia. But would I ever be able to afford it? Even if the home was much smaller, the land would be priced at a premium. And though I was a member of House Tavarian, and my shop was doing a brisk business, I did not have the purse that a lord of Fanuel's means did.

"So what period of history are you researching?" Fanuel said once we'd taken the edge off our hunger. "You said you were from Warosia. Is it the witch wars? That was a fascinating, if bloody, time period for your country."

"Actually, I am studying Elantian history," Salcombe said. "Specifically, the Dragon War. I am writing a treatise on the history of the mages who subdued the dragon god, and was hoping you might help me fill in some salient details."

Salcombe proceeded to cite several of the mage families involved, which impressed Fanuel, as this was information that only mages would know. My heart sank as he gave fairly specific details—it seemed that Salcombe had gotten quite far, tracing back three families. He'd obviously gotten to the source of at least one, since he had a piece of heart, and far enough with Tavarian's own mage ancestry that he'd correctly guessed the second location. The third family, theTimmermans, were the ones mentioned in the diary Salcombe and I had found, and from the way Fanuel's eyes flickered in recognition when the name was brought up, I knew Salcombe was right on the money about his involvement.

And yet, there was no hint of a dragon heart relic around. Which meant it was either very well shielded, or Fanuel didn't have it.

"Of course, the dragon heart story is merely a legend," Salcombe was saying, "but it is a fascinating one, and the families I have unearthed thus far seem to be real. It may be that there is some relic the five of them destroyed or hid together, though of course I am not in the relic-hunting business. My interest is merely academic."

"Merely a legend?" Lord Fanuel laughed. "On the contrary, the dragon god heart is quite real. One of my own forebears, who was descended from the Timmermans, was charged with guarding one of the pieces."

"Really?" Salcombe leaned in, his eyes bright with interest. As he did, his hand flicked over Lord Fanuel's bowl of lobster bisque, the movement so fast I wouldn't have caught it if I hadn't been watching. "How do you know the piece is real? Have you seen it yourself?"

"No," Fanuel admitted. He ate another spoonful of bisque before continuing. "I do not know where my ancestors hid it. It was over two thousand years ago, after all. Besides, some things are best left forgotten, and a piece of the god who nearly destroyed our world is certainly one of them."

"Agreed," Salcombe said, but the zeal in his eyes said otherwise. "Even so, it seems quite shocking that your family would have lost such an important relic. How are you to know that someone hasn't gotten their hands on it, if it does indeed exist?"

"I didn't say it was lost," Fanuel said, his voice coloring with insult. The drug Salcombe had put into his stew was taking effect, loosening his emotions and his tongue. "Merely that I do not know where it is hidden. I am not in contact with the branch of my family that is involved, as they live in Dardil."

"Where do they live, exactly?"

Using the help of the truth serum, Salcombe deftly extracted the information from Fanuel. As it turned out, the last member of this particular branch of Fanuel's family that he'd seen was his cousin Helumar Toppenfeld, who had died over ten years ago. He'd lived in Triul, a village some four miles south of Lange, Dardil's capital.

"Did your cousin die of natural causes?" Salcombe asked.

"As far as I know, yes," Fanuel said. "He was very old, over three hundred years. It was his time to go."

"How old are you?" I blurted out before I could stop myself. I'd heard that mages lived extraordinarily long lives, longer than even dragon riders, but I had no idea some of them could live for centuries!

"A little over one hundred years old," Fanuel said. His gaze sharpened on me with interest, the tiny drop of serum Salcombe had given him already beginning to wear off. "What do you think about all this talk of dragons and mages, Lady Zara? Do you share the same interests as your husband?"

"My wife is very good to indulge my passions and curiosities," Salcombe cut in before I could answer. "To make it up to her, I make sure we attend the finest parties wherever we are traveling, and allow her to buy most anything she wants." He patted my hand fondly, ever the doting husband, and I buried my scowl.

"Is that right?" Fanuel asked. "You must have spent time in King Zoltar's court. What did you think?"

"It was...different," I said. "The king seems to be very open with his affections, and the people are more interested in gossip than state affairs." I described my presentation at court, and the garden party afterward. "I must admit that the altercation between the Zallabarian ambassador and the king was quite thrilling, though also terrifying. I don't understand why the king banished my husband and me. I feel as though I was in the wrong place at the wrong time."

Fanuel shook his head, both sympathetic and disgusted. "You remind me of why I never go to court," he said. "Those social circles have always been a waste of time for me—my countrymen are so irrational about magic, even the king. If the war with Elantia is off, so much the better. We should concentrate on our navy and let the continental powers fight among themselves instead of sending our own young men off to die."

"A surprisingly sensible attitude," Salcombe said, and I privately agreed. So sensible, in fact, that I wondered if I should try to pull Fanuel aside privately and ask him for help. I could tell him that I was a hostage and warn him what Salcombe was really up to—after all, Fanuel would have never divulged so much information to him without the truth serum.

But as Salcombe steered the conversation back to history, I realized the risk was too great. He and Fanuel seemed to be hitting it off so well, would the old mage even believe me? If I told the truth, I might find myself treated as an Elantian spy yet again, and I had no desire to risk the gallows. No, it was better to rely on myself. Dardil was a neutral country, a much safer place to make a break for it than here. I would accompany Salcombe, and once we were out of enemy territory, I would figure out how to free myself from him once and for all.

SEVEN

Salcombe and I stayed a little while longer at Fanuel's estate, taking a tour of his private library and continuing to talk about history and magic. I strongly suspected the only reason we stayed as long as we did was to avert any lingering suspicion Fanuel might have, for the moment Fanuel announced that he had business to attend to, Salcombe was more than happy to take his leave.

"That visit was well worth these weeks of putting up with the Traggaran nobility," Salcombe said effusively as the carriage took us back down the cliff. "If the piece of heart is in Dardil, that will make our task easier, as we won't need to constantly look over our shoulders. Though we will continue to use the Trentiano alias."

"When are we leaving for Dardil?" I asked, my mind whirling. Would there be time to sneak a letter to Tavarian via the inn's outgoing post, informing him of my next destination? We hadn't been gone long, and there was a good chance I could get a message to him before he concluded his business with the king.

"Tonight, if possible," Salcombe said. "Trolbos and I will go to the docks immediately to procure passage. It should only take us two days and nights, provided that the winds are in our favor."

*Damn.* That would give me no time at all.

We took refuge at an inn close to the harbor, and Salcombe booked two rooms for us. The moment we were settled, Salcombe and Trolbos took off for the docks, leaving me with Hickam. As before, the luggage was stowed in the second guard's room, but it didn't take long before I heard him leave, likely heading down to the common room for food and drink. My efforts at being helpful and submissive were paying off—the guard wasn't nearly as vigilant as Trolbos would have been.

*This is it, Zara. Your chance to take back what's yours.*

Heart pounding, I approached the adjoining door between our rooms, and used one of my hairpins to jiggle the lock. The mechanism slid free, and I carefully opened the door, scanning the room for any sign of the guard just in case I'd been mistaken. The moment I was sure the room was empty, I hurried inside, shutting the door behind me.

It took no time at all for me to find the bag where my belongings were stowed—my treasure sense led me straight to them. I nearly crowed with jubilation as my hand closed around the hilt of the dragon blade, and if it hadn't been a deadly sharp weapon, I would have cuddled it to my chest like a teddy bear. I took an indulgent moment to spin the weapon in my hand, the blades shooting out to their full length with a single thought, then retracting. I made them as short as they could get, then wrapped the weapon in a silk scarf and tucked it into one of my skirt pockets. My goggles and lockpicks went into the other pocket, and my knives went into my spelled boots, which I'd slipped gratefully onto my feet, all too happy to ditch the useless silk slippers I'd been forced to wear.

I zipped up the bag and started to stand up, ready to get out of there before the guard returned. But my treasure sense itched, reminding me of the elixir that was squirreled away in one of these bags. I rummaged through the luggage, unearthing a leather satchel with a lock on it. I used my lockpick to open it, then pulled out a glass vial of silvery liquid—the same liquid I'd seen Salcombe's acolytes drinking in the catacombs. It was definitely the dragon god elixir!

Briefly, I entertained the idea of getting rid of it, but I knew that Salcombe would notice its absence immediately, and I would be the prime suspect. Reluctantly, I put the vial back. My fingers brushed against a small leather pouch as I did so, and my treasure sense pinged urgently.

I opened the pouch to find several locks of red hair.

"Ha!" I punched the air with one hand even as I used my other to stuff the hair down my bodice. This was even better than the weapons! Without my hair, Salcombe wouldn't be able to track me. Should I make a run for it now, while he and Trolbos were still out?

Stowing the luggage, I rushed back to my room and locked the door, then stole out into the hall. Conversation and laughter drifted up the stairs, but I didn't dare go out that way— Salcombe's guard would see me. Instead, I went the other direction, up a second set of stairs and into the attic. It was a bit of a struggle to get onto the roof with my skirts hampering me, but I managed to squeeze out of the window to survey the city from above.

Unfortunately, Salcombe had chosen exactly the wrong location for me. This close to the docks, the streets were teeming with drunken sailors who wouldn't hesitate to take advantage of a finely dressed lady. If I'd had normal clothes I could try to escape via rooftop, but these stupid dresses made it impossible to get around, and the ground wasn't safe for a woman to travel alone at night. City guards patrolled the streets, sending a chill up my spine. News that the war had been called off would not have reached this town yet, and it was entirely possible the guards were still on alert for Elantian spies.

I was about to climb down from the roof when the bond suddenly flared to life in my mind. *"Lessie?"* I cried, my heart jumping into my throat.

*"Zara!"* Lessie's voice was faint but clear. *"Where are you? Are you all right?"*

*"I'm fine,"* I said, tears of joy spilling down my cheeks. *"I've been trying to reach you for days! What is going on? I've sensed your anger, and it's been driving me crazy not knowing what's wrong."*

*"Oh, Zara, it's been terrible,"* Lessie said, and my heart squeezed at her plaintive tone. *"Colonel Roche is very angry with you for not coming back, and they think that you have caused Carvin and Hallus's deaths. There is a rumor circling that Hallus's head was mounted on a pike in the Traggaran capital as a trophy, and that you were seen consorting with the*

enemy. The colonel and the major are convinced that you are a traitor and a deserter, and will court-martial you the moment you return." She hesitated. "Is it true what they say, about the head?"

"Yes," I said gently. Lessie's pain and grief swelled inside the bond, and fresh tears pricked at my eyes. "But I wasn't consorting with the enemy, Lessie." I gave her a full account of what had happened between me and Salcombe since reaching the capital, and where I was now.

"So the Traggarans have decided to bow out of the war after all?" Lessie asked when I finished, sounding elated for the first time. "Tavarian is right, Zara—you are a hero, and the moment Colonel Roche hears of this, she will have to let you go. I told Kadryn the truth about what happened to us, and he has relayed the account to Jallis, but Roche will not even entertain him. I believe she is prejudiced against dragon riders, which is absurd," Lessie added with a huff. "A woman like her should never have been put in charge."

I relaxed a little—Lessie was starting to sound like her old self. Whatever was being done to her had not damaged her mind. "I agree, but I don't care what Colonel Roche thinks of me. Has she harmed you?"

"Not harmed, per se," Lessie said, though the heat in her tone suggested otherwise. "But I am only allowed to fly twice a week to maintain the strength in my wings, under heavy guard from dragons three times my size. The rest of the time I am shackled and drugged. The hope is that you will eventually come back to rescue me."

"Shackled and drugged?" White-hot fury blazed through me at the image my mind conjured of Lessie chained in her stall, listless from whatever drug they were pumping into her. *"You can't break free?"*

*"The shackles are made of some unbreakable alloy, magically reinforced,"* Lessie said bitterly. *"Even my dragon fire won't melt them."*

*"Dragon's balls,"* I swore, so angry I could hardly see. No wonder Lessie had been so distraught! I wanted to storm back to the military camp and string Colonel Roche up by her toes, then use my lockpicks to break Lessie out and fly away. But there was no way I could storm the camp by myself, and without Tavarian to back me up, I would end up in military prison.

*"If you are leaving for Dardil tonight, then we cannot wait for Tavarian to make it back here to testify on your behalf,"* Lessie said, reading my thoughts. *"I will have to escape and come to you. I am due for an exercise flight tomorrow night—I can slip my escort and come straight to you."*

*"I don't want you to put yourself at risk—"*

*"Zara, we are both at risk every day you remain in Salcombe's hands,"* Lessie interrupted. *"He may be treating you nicely, but the moment he gets his hands on another piece of heart, the dragon god's influence will corrupt him again. He will kill us once he gets what he wants. You may not want to admit that, but that is the only way this will end."*

My chest tightened as an unexpected wave of grief hit me. *"You're right,"* I said, looking down at the street again. *"Maybe I should take off now, before he gets back. I can try to sneak onto a boat, or maybe you can meet me—"*

*"No,"* Lessie said. *"I would do anything for you, Zara, but flying back to Traggar's shores would be suicide for me, and*

*possibly Tavarian. I don't know much about politics, but I don't think the Traggaran king would take kindly to dragons flying over his lands while our countries are trying to broker peace."*

"Shit." I hadn't even thought of that, but Lessie was right. Her dragon wisdom was growing by the day, despite her young age, and once again I was impressed by how insightful and intelligent these creatures were. *"You're right, but Dardil isn't going to be safer either. They're neutral, which means that if they see you flying over the city they'll have to shoot at you on principle, or Zallabar will think they've allied with Elantia."* That was the price of neutrality, I thought morosely. Although the intent was to stay out of war, in reality it meant making everyone involved a potential enemy.

*"Then I'll pick you up before you arrive."*

I blinked. *"From the ship?"*

*"Why not?"* I could sense Lessie's grin. *"Just sneak up to the deck and I'll grab you before anyone knows what's happening. Think of it, Zara. Once we're reunited, the two of us can go anywhere. Maybe we'll leave all these idiots behind and join Muza overseas."*

Normally, Lessie's excitement would have been infectious, but I found myself sighing at her childish outlook. *"It is not so easy as that,"* I said. *"If I flee without clearing my name, then I will be branded as a criminal and we will never be able to return home."*

*"Is it truly a home when your own peers turn on you so easily?"* Lessie countered. But I could tell that my point had been taken seriously. *"I admit that I do not want to leave the friends I have made behind, and neither do you. We need only stay away*

*long enough for Tavarian to return so he can clear your name. Perhaps we'll wait for him at his secret estate. Surely he will stop by there at some point, or we can get word to him from there."*

"That's a good idea," I told her. *"But let's focus on escaping first. We can decide what to do once I'm free."*

I wished I could stay up on the roof all night and talk to Lessie, but some instinct made me look down. My pulse jumped as I spotted Salcombe and Trolbos walking back from the docks, and I quickly ducked back into the window and headed downstairs. I needed to get back to my room before Salcombe or his flunkies noticed my absence. I only needed to survive them for one more night, and there was no way I would blow things now, not when I was so close to freedom I could practically taste it.

EIGHT

The next morning, Salcombe and I boarded a small merchant ship bound for Dardil. The one passenger ship had been completely full, but Salcombe and Trolbos had booked passage by offering the merchant a bribe hefty enough that the man had given us the captain's cabin for the duration of our stay. Salcombe was in a cheery mood as we sailed across the relatively calm waters, but a tension headache throbbed at my temples. I'd barely caught a wink of sleep last night, fearing that one of the guards would go through the luggage and find that I'd stolen my things back. The luggage was safely stored below deck, out of my reach, but even now tension dug into my shoulders. What if Salcombe called for one of his elixirs? I wished now that I'd had the presence of mind to dilute the vials with water, but it was too late now.

But as the day went on, and the sun crept closer and closer to the horizon, I relaxed. Salcombe seemed content, and though Trolbos fixed me with his usual glare, it was with no more suspicion than usual. None of them suspected that my weapons and tools were concealed beneath my day dress—my knives were tucked into my boots, and my skirt and chemise were thick enough no one could see the outline of the hilts or the tops of the boots. I wished I had a proper sheath for the dragon blade as well, rather than the silk I'd wrapped it in, but there was nothing for it. At least I didn't have to worry about unwrapping it to use it—the blades would cut right through the cloth the moment I extended them.

The seas remained fairly calm throughout the day, but as night settled in, the boat began to rock more. Soon enough, rain started to pelt the deck, and the captain sent the four of us indoors. "Don't need no land-leggers getting in the way," he said gruffly as he ushered Salcombe and me into the cabin, and Trolbos and Hickam to the sailors' quarters, where they slept on hammocks. "This only looks to be a minor squall, but the ocean's a fickle beast. We might find ourselves in a nasty storm later."

My stomach churned. "I hate this," I said to Salcombe as I sat on a chair bolted into a corner of the room. "What if we end up locked in here, and the ship starts sinking?" The memory of those poor sailors who'd been robbed and locked up in their own cargo hold to drown slammed into my brain, and I shivered.

"That isn't going to happen," Salcombe assured me. "Trolbos and Hickam are more than capable of getting us out, and I have faith in the captain. These men sail through rough waters regularly—the channel is always being hit by squalls. We will be fine."

I sucked in a deep breath. *Fine.* I'm sure those men had

been seasoned sailors as well, and yet if Lessie and I hadn't found them, they would have died. Then again, Lessie *was* on her way to get me, or at least she would be if she could escape from her escort. Now that night had fallen, it was only a matter of hours until Lessie left the stables for her midnight flight.

With nothing better to do to pass the time, I made a makeshift bed on the floor with a pillow and the spare blanket, and curled up for a nap. The rocking boat made it hard to sleep, but I tried to doze, knowing this would be my only chance to get some rest. Salcombe stayed up for a while, reading by the light of the candle on the bedside table. It took a few hours, but eventually the sound of his snores filled the cabin, and the candle-light flickered out.

*"Zara!"* My eyes popped open at the sound of Lessie's voice in my head, clearer than before. Was it midnight already? *"I'm coming to you now."*

*"You've already managed to escape?"*

*"Yes."* Lessie sounded incredibly smug. *"We have excellent cloud cover tonight, so it wasn't very hard. I'm going to double back, try to confuse the trail, before I head your way. I'll be there within the hour."*

Excitement surged through me. I wanted to jump up and race out the door, dance and wave my arms around like a crazy person. Instead I moved toward the door on silent feet, thankful I'd stolen back my spelled boots. The creaky floorboards made no sound as I snuck onto the deck, leaving Salcombe snoring away behind me.

To my relief, the rains had passed. The boat still rocked a bit, but nothing like the swells we'd felt earlier. I imagined

Trolbos had spent most of the squall permanently bent over a bucket, and I smirked. He wouldn't be coming out anytime soon, which was even better.

Glancing up, I thought about climbing up the mast and into the crow's nest, which would be a perfect vantage point from which to jump on Lessie's back. But there were still a few crew members up on deck, and I didn't want to draw undue attention. Instead, I leaned against the starboard railing and took a deep breath of fresh ocean air, the wind running its ghostly fingers through my hair and clearing my head.

Where would Lessie and I go once we were reunited? The hidden valley seemed like the best choice, but we would have to be careful. The military would be on the lookout for us, and Salcombe could always show up again, now that he knew the location. We would have to get past the encampment on the channel, avoid the patrols that would be looking for us. If they caught us, Lessie and I would both be imprisoned, and I would be court-martialed.

Of course, we were on the verge of war, which meant my court-martial wasn't the highest priority. It was quite possible we'd be left to languish for a while, and that Tavarian would come to our aid before any decisions were made. But what if he didn't? What if things went wrong with Traggar? King Zoltar had already proven to be as capricious as the rumors said—someone at court could easily put a bug in his ear about Tavarian and get him executed. A chill raced up my spine at the thought. What if I never saw him again?

*One thing at a time,* I told myself. I focused on the bond, my spirits lifting as I sensed Lessie's presence. She was getting closer by the minute. *"How far are you?"*

*"Fifteen minutes o—"*

I stiffened as a sense of alarm hit me. *"Lessie?"* I cried through the bond, tightening my grip on the rail. I searched the skies for any sign of her, but the clouds were so thick I could barely see anything despite the large moon hanging overhead. *"Lessie, what's happening?"*

*"Get out of sight!"*

The panic in Lessie's voice drove all questions out of my mind. Without hesitation, I raced below deck, uncaring if the sailors saw me. Any danger to my life was also a danger to Lessie's. Heart pounding, I shut myself in a mop closet, straining to read Lessie's thoughts. But they were all jumbled up by a wave of bitter anger and disappointment.

*"Lessie,"* I called again, trying not to let my own panic overwhelm me. *"What's happening?"*

*"It was a trap,"* she said morosely. I could feel her moving away, and my stomach sank. *"My two escorts have been following me this entire time. I can only imagine they were hoping I would lead them straight to you."*

Dammit. *"Are you all right?"* I demanded. *"Did they catch you?"*

*"Not yet,"* she said fiercely. Her presence receded faster, and I could tell that she was on the run.

*"Wait,"* I said, desperation filling me. *"Come back, Lessie. Maybe it's better this way if they take us."* Despite my misgivings about being captured, I couldn't bear the idea of this continued separation. The ache in my heart seemed to grow with every

yard of distance she put between us. How long until I wouldn't be able to communicate with her at all?

"No," Lessie said. *"They are very angry with me now. If we go back, the two of us will both be punished for treason, and I refuse to submit to such treatment when neither of us has done anything wrong. I will evade them, then come back for you when it is safe."*

I sagged against the wall, ignoring the broom handle jabbing into my back. Was there ever going to be a safe place for either of us? By tomorrow night, Salcombe and I would be in Dardil. Perhaps that was a good thing, as it would be extremely risky for the other dragons to follow her there, but Lessie would be in more danger than ever. At least in Elantia, she would have no risk of being shot down. Tears of grief and frustration filled my eyes, and I clenched my fists.

*"I'm sorry, Zara."* Lessie's voice was growing fainter, but the misery in it was clear. *"I've failed you."*

"No," I said gently. *"You didn't fail me at all. You did exactly the right thing. I'm the one who's failed you. I should have ignored Carvis's orders and headed back to the mainland instead of blindly obeying. We would have been reprimanded, but we wouldn't be in this mess."*

*"Maybe, but if you hadn't ended up in the Traggaran capital, you wouldn't have been able to thwart the Traggar-Zallabar alliance,"* Lessie pointed out. *"We'll get through this, Zara. I promise."*

I smiled through my tears. *"You're right."* Reaching through the bond, I gave her a mental hug. *"I'll see you soon. Love you."*

*"Love you, too."*

The last word faded away, and I knew that she was beyond reach. A few tears fell, but I wiped them away, then headed back to the cabin I shared with Salcombe. Standing over his bedside, watching the rise and fall of his thin chest, I was struck by the violent urge to drive my dragon blade through his heart and end this threat once and for all. Gritting my teeth, I raised the weapon overhead, extending the blades out a few inches. Just one downward strike, and this would all be over.

*And then what?* a voice, likely the voice of reason, whispered in my head. *Are you willing to kill the entire crew too?* Because I would have to, or at least tie them up and steer the entire ship myself. It would be one thing if it were only Salcombe and his henchmen around, another thing entirely to have to fight off an entire crew of sailors. The captain wouldn't listen to my excuses—his word was law aboard the ship, and he would have me imprisoned and turned over to the authorities the moment we docked to be tried for murder. I didn't know how that worked, exactly, since neither Salcombe or I were from Dardil, but I was sure they had some kind of procedure for this situation, and I couldn't risk execution or Lessie would die, too.

Sighing, I lowered my blade and tucked it away. Killing Salcombe was, ultimately, the right thing to do. But a secret part of me was glad that, at least for now, I would have to stay my hand.

NINE

After one more day and night on the ship, we finally arrived at Lange. I gripped the railing as the ship slowly docked, reaching out with my senses for Lessie. She hadn't come back last night, and I could only imagine that meant she was still in danger. Had the dragons managed to catch her after all, and bring her back to Elantia? But no, she wasn't far enough away to account for that. She must have found some other place to take refuge.

"A beautiful city," Salcombe said. I started—I was so tired I hadn't realized he'd come to stand next to me. His eyes glittered as he surveyed the capital, which sprawled before us in a buzz of color and activity. Lange was ringed by tree-lined boulevards rather than a defensive wall, and bisected by the Sulae River, around which the city had sprung up nearly eight hundred years ago. From here, I could see past the bustling marina and the city center to the residential areas, and the older buildings on the west side and the manicured lawns and restored townhouses on the east told me that the city was divided by more than just a body of water. "I've never taken you here, have I?"

I shook my head. "Dardil was never high on your list of priorities."

"A mistake," he said softly. "One we will be rectifying immediately, thanks to Lord Fanuel." He smiled as the crew lowered the gangplank and offered his arm to me. "Are you ready, Mrs. Trentiano?"

Steeling myself, I took Salcombe's arm and allowed him to steer me through the marina and to the street, where he immediately hired a hansom. We found lodgings at an inn near the city center—nothing luxurious, since we were Mr. and Mrs. again, rather than lord and lady, but still much nicer than anything I would have booked on my own. Part of me wanted nothing more than to flop down on the very comfortable-looking bed, but Salcombe insisted on breakfast so we could listen to the local gossip and read the papers. To my disgust, we were joined by Trolbos, while Hickam stayed behind to watch over our belongings. By some miracle, no one had noticed that I'd stolen back my weapons and gotten rid of the hair Salcombe had taken from me, but how long would that last? I needed to escape as soon as possible.

Salcombe ordered a large breakfast and asked the server to bring him all of the local papers for today. Over copious amounts of coffee—which I desperately needed—the two of us went through the papers together, while Trolbos alternated between scanning our surroundings for any threats and glaring at me. Normally, I would have been tempted to glare back, but I hardly noticed—the news was far more alarming than I'd anticipated.

"So Zallabar has officially declared war, eh?" Salcombe said, sitting back in his chair. Unlike me, he seemed relaxed, almost satisfied. "I must say I'm surprised, considering they've lost both Quoronis and Traggar as allies. They must be very confident in their military if they are willing to go it alone anyway."

"You don't seem very concerned that our fellow countrymen are about to be attacked," I said, my voice an acid bite. I knew I shouldn't react this way to Salcombe's nonchalance, but I couldn't help myself. "By the time we come home after scouring the world for the pieces of the dragon god's heart, Elantia might very well be renamed New Zallabar."

Salcombe scoffed. "I don't intend for this hunt to take nearly as long as you think," he said. "Once I have all the pieces and have resurrected the god, nothing will be able to stand in our way. Do you really think Zallabar's military stands a chance against Zakyiar's might? We will be able to conquer *all* our enemies, Zara."

I swallowed at the fanatical gleam in Salcombe's eyes. The zealot was back, eroding the common sense and cool logic that my mentor prized above all else. I wanted to grab his shoulders and shake him, to scream in his ear that the dragon god wouldn't care about Salcombe's wants, that once he was free he would do whatever he pleased and no one would be able to stop him. That a god who had been imprisoned for thousands of years wouldn't consider Zallabar to be his enemy, but Elantia. He was dooming his own people to death for the sake of greed and power.

But I knew that my words wouldn't reach Salcombe.

Despite the rocky sea journey we'd just endured, he was flushed with the glow of health, strong and vibrant. He had to have taken more of the elixir. Judging by the frequency, it looked like he needed to replenish every two to three days. How would he get more, once he was out? If I could get free and track down Red Beard, could I cut Salcombe off from his supply? He would be forced to slow down quite a bit if he was weakened—before he'd started this mad journey of his, before I'd decided to go independent and open up the Treasure Trove, he'd been sending me out on hunts for him because he'd grown too sick to go himself.

*No wonder the power of the dragon god is so appealing to him,* I thought, feeling an unexpected pang of sympathy. If I were confined to my house by illness, never again to be allowed to travel the world and hunt for treasure, I would lose my mind. To what lengths would I go to restore my own strength?

*Not this,* I told myself fiercely. *Never this.* Because unlike Salcombe, I didn't think that my life was more important than anyone else's. I could never risk the lives of thousands—no, *millions*—for the sake of my own happiness. And *that* had nothing to do with the dragon god's influence, and everything to do with Salcombe's cold, selfish nature.

I had to stop thinking of him as a victim.

"Aha," Salcombe said, setting his paper down. He jabbed at an advertisement in the classified section. "This woman should help us on our search for Toppenfeld."

I leaned in to read the advertisement. It was from an agency that, amongst other things, specialized in tracing people's genealogies. "By appointment only," I read aloud. "That should take some time, shouldn't it?"

But Salcombe flashed a smile. "I find that with a sufficient amount of coin, one can usually move one's name up any list quite quickly."

Now that Salcombe had a lead, he ushered us through breakfast, then we set off for the agency. The address was not far from the inn, only a ten-minute walk to a small, brick building perched on a corner in what appeared to be the business district of the capital. The brass sign hanging from the awning proclaimed it to be the Kingsley Agency.

Salcombe knocked on the green door, and an elderly woman opened it, dressed in a high-waisted skirt and white blouse that was so heavily starched it was nearly as stiff as her posture. "May I help you?" she asked, peering through her spectacles.

"Mrs. Kingsley, I presume?" Salcombe gave her a charming smile. "My name is Pieri Trentiano, and this is my wife, Zara. The two of us are tracing back her lineage, as she has ancestors from Dardil, and we were hoping you could help. We are prepared to pay handsomely," he added, his hand surreptitiously moving to the purse tied to his belt.

"Ancestors?" Mrs. Kingsley pushed her spectacles higher on her nose, scrutinizing me with keen gray eyes. "Yes, I believe you do have some Dardilian in you, particularly in the slant of your nose. Very well, you may come in."

Salcombe and I exchanged surprised looks—he might have discovered the identity of my parents, but he clearly hadn't traced my lineage far back enough to a foreign country. Perhaps there was a distant cousin or aunt in my family tree from Dardil,

I thought as we followed her in. Resisting the urge to touch my nose—which was perfectly straight, and not at all unusual, or so I'd always assumed—I followed Mrs. Kingsley into her office, behind Salcombe. Trolbos was right on my heels, as usual, practically breathing down my neck. My fingers itched with the need to stab my dragon blade into the side of his neck, one of the only parts of his body that was unprotected thanks to his chain mail armor. But murdering him in a genteel woman's house wasn't going to earn me any points with the Dardilian authorities, so I refrained.

Mrs. Kingsley walked behind her desk and offered seats to Salcombe and me. She dismissed Trolbos as a manservant, and he took up a position near the door.

"Would you care for any coffee or tea?" she asked briskly.

"No, thank you," Salcombe said before I could answer. "We are eager to get started."

"Very well," Mrs. Kingsley said. She turned that keen gaze back to me. "What information do you have about your ancestor?" she asked me. "And how many generations back does this relationship go?"

Briefly, I considered telling the truth: that I had no relations in Dardil at all, and that Salcombe was forcing me to help him track down this family so he could steal from them. But Trolbos's glare was affixed to the back of my neck, and I had no desire to give him any excuse to lash out at me. This woman might come off as a bit snooty, but she didn't deserve to get caught in the crossfire, and I knew that if Trolbos and I got into a fight, it would be an epic showdown.

"I'm not sure of her given name," I said, "but my great-great-

great-grandmother was a Toppenfeld. I traced the name back, and it seems to come from Dardil."

"Indeed, it does!" The old woman smiled, her reserved manner falling away. "The Toppenfelds are a very distinguished, though extinct, family. They lived in and around Lange for close to a thousand years before their last scion passed away."

"Extinct?" I could practically taste Salcombe's disappointment, which he didn't even attempt to hide. "There are no relatives at all?"

"I'm afraid not," Mrs. Kingsley said. She rose and selected an old leather tome from one of the shelves behind her and brought it back to the desk. "Helumar Toppenfeld was the last of his line, and he passed away nearly ten years ago," she said, opening the book up to the Toppenfeld family tree. "Yes, I'm afraid he had no children."

"What about marriages?" Salcombe asked.

"None on record," she said. There was a glint in her eye as she looked at me. "The Toppenfelds were rumored to have magical talent, you know."

"Really?" I widened my eyes, pretending surprise. "I didn't know that. No one in my family has ever had magic."

"That is not too surprising," Mrs. Kingsley said. "Your link to the Toppenfelds is several generations old. Although I must say, I don't recall any Warosian marriages on record." She picked up a magnifying glass and bent closer to the family tree.

"Mrs. Kingsley," Salcombe interrupted before she could chase down that line of inquiry. "What happened to the Toppenfeld family estate? My wife and I were looking forward to meeting her relatives, but if there are none left alive, perhaps it might be possible to at least retrieve a memento or heirloom of sorts so she can stay connected to that branch of the family."

"Oh, the estate has long been sold off," Mrs. Kingsley said with a wave of her hand. "But the new owners, the Lenarts, are nice people, and you might be able to convince them to give you a tour of the place if you explain the family connection. They may have kept some of the original furniture and art, and if you find something you like, they may be willing to part with it for a price."

"Thank you." Salcombe opened his purse and set a hefty amount of coin on the table. "Would you be willing to provide the address?"

"Most certainly."

Finished, Salcombe and I left the agency before the woman could ask more questions and expose us for the frauds we were. "Just as Lord Fanuel told us," Salcombe said as we walked back to the hotel. Mrs. Kingsley had given us an address that was outside the village of Triul, as well as a copy of the Toppenfeld family tree, dating back for the last four hundred years. "We are nearing the end of this leg of the hunt, Zara. I can feel it in my bones."

I said nothing, knowing in my heart that he was right. Mrs. Kingsley had told us, to my dismay, that Toppenfeld hadn't traveled much and did not own any other estates. If she was correct—and she seemed quite knowledgeable—then this was likely where the piece of heart was hidden. Of course, it was entirely possible that the Toppenfelds had a hidden estate, like Tavarian, and had chosen to sequester the artifact there. But then again, Tavarian had kept his at his primary residence, close to home, where he could keep an eye on it. The Toppenfelds likely would have done the same.

The moment we returned to the inn, Salcombe hired a carriage to take us to Triul. The hour-long carriage ride passed slowly, the tension-filled silence hanging thick in the air. My fingers itched to draw my blade, but I didn't know if I could fight my way out of the carriage in such close quarters. I might be armed, but Trolbos bristled with weapons. I'd counted them on more than one occasion—he had hidden retractable blades tucked into his sleeves, the sword strapped to his waist, and a dozen knives strapped in various places on his body. Hickam had stayed behind to watch the belongings, so it was a two-on-one fight, something that the old me would have risked in a heartbeat.

But I didn't have only my life to consider anymore. I had to think about Lessie, too.

"Here we are," Salcombe said as we approached the estate. He tapped on the hood and ordered the driver to stop outside the walls, out of view of the front gates.

I frowned. "We're not going to go inside?"

"There is no need," Salcombe said. "You can sense the heart from here, can you not?"

The moment he said the words, my treasure sense activated instantly. My blood went cold as that distinctive *gong* reverberated in my skull, and I hastily turned the noise down before I gave in to the urge to clutch my head.

But Salcombe had seen the flash of pain on my face. "So, it

is here," he said smugly. He looked at Trolbos. "Our hard work and patience are finally paying off."

"Yes, they are." Trolbos grinned at me, as if he could sense my despair.

"I don't know that it's the heart," I said, grasping at straws. "It could be something else."

Salcombe smiled. "Then we'd best find out for certain, shouldn't we?" He tapped the roof again and ordered the carriage to head back to Lange. "We will go back to the inn to rest and prepare. Tonight, we will come back and search the estate thoroughly."

My stomach churned as the carriage rumbled back down the road. How was I going to get out of this? Maybe I could sneak back to the estate on my own, try to dig up the heart, and run away with it before Salcombe could come back. Now that I'd recovered the hair Salcombe had stolen from me, he wouldn't be able to track me again. Or maybe I could send a warning to the family that had bought the Toppenfeld estate...but they had no idea they were sitting on a valuable magical artifact that had the potential to destroy the world. They would likely think me crazy and ignore any of my attempts to reach out.

We walked back into the inn, my mind racing. Was Lessie near? I reached through the bond, trying to gauge the distance. She was closer now, but not close enough for a retrieval.

"You are considering escape," Salcombe said in a low voice as we walked through the lobby, "so you will stay in Trolbos's room for the remainder of the day, rather than mine. If you so much as look toward the doors or windows, I will have him snap your neck."

White-hot rage whipped through me, and I reached into my skirt pocket for my dragon blade. If Salcombe was going to cut off all my options and make it impossible for Lessie to rescue me, what difference did it make anymore? I might as well eliminate him.

But before I could, someone stepped in front of us.

"Zara!" Jallis beamed, and I nearly toppled over in shock. He was wearing civilian clothes—crisp white shirt, tan trousers, and a pair of brown leather boots paired with a matching coat. "It's so wonderful to see you again!"

He threw his arms around me in a hug, and I returned the embrace. His alpine air and woodsmoke smell wrapped around me, and I had to fight against the instinct to bury my face in his familiar warmth. "What are you doing here?" I asked, fear and elation racing through me. Was Jallis here as friend or foe?

"Yes, what *are* you doing here?" Salcombe asked from next to me. I didn't have to look at him to know that he was furious— his glacial tone spoke volumes.

"I'm afraid I've business to discuss with Zara," Jallis said as he withdrew from me. His tone was apologetic, but there was no mistaking the hard glint in his eyes. "Would you mind giving us a moment to speak in private, Mr. Trentiano?"

Salcombe's eyes flashed. So Jallis had tracked us here and had been around long enough to get the name of our alias. I saw Trolbos move in, prepared to strike with one of his hidden blades, but Salcombe jerked his head to the left in the tiniest of motions. There were far too many witnesses here for either of them to afford to make a scene.

"Certainly," Salcombe said, hiding his fury behind a pleasant smile. "Take all the time you need."

Jallis offered me his arm, leading me to a grouping of couches near the entrance. Salcombe retreated to the other side of the lobby, but Trolbos took up a spot next to the door, blocking our exit. Even so, he was only one man, hulking and dangerous as he might be. Jallis and I couldn't kill him, but we might be able to overpower him and escape before Salcombe could call for his other guard.

We sat down, and I immediately ordered coffee from a server who came by to help us. "What are you doing here?" I asked again, keeping my voice low. "How did you find me?"

"What do you think, Zara? That we wouldn't be tracking your every move?" Frustration brimmed in Jallis's eyes as he leaned in. "An informant told us that you were coming here to Dardil, so I followed you here. If Dardil wasn't neutral territory, Colonel Roche would have sent a team to bring you back. She's already called for you to be court-martialed."

"For what, exactly?" I hissed. I dug my nails into my thighs to keep from grabbing Jallis by the front of his shirt. I'd known there was a rift between us, but was he really as stupid as everyone else? "You know I'm not a deserter. Lessie told you and Kadryn what happened!"

Jallis sighed heavily. "And I believe her. But Roche and the others are certain that you've deserted, leaving your dragon behind to consort with the enemy. The fact that you've been traveling with a strange man and came to Dardil instead of going back to Elantia isn't helping, either."

I curled my lip. "That man is Salcombe, in disguise, and I didn't have any choice."

"Salcombe?" Jallis swiveled his head around to look at Salcombe, then back at me. "What do you mean, you didn't have a choice? How did you even end up with him?"

"It's a long story." But I sighed at the look on Jallis's face and told him everything—that I'd gone to the capital to seek out Tavarian, and had been rescued from the gallows by Salcombe. The anger on Jallis's face softened into sympathy, then amazement, as I gave him the basic details of my time at court, and how I'd managed to avert the Traggar-Zallabar alliance.

"The only reason I'm still with Salcombe is because he offered a safe way for me to escape Traggar, and because he's held both my and Lessie's lives in his hands," I whispered fiercely. "He and his henchmen drink an elixir distilled from the power of the dragon heart piece he has that makes them incredibly strong, almost invulnerable. I haven't found a way to break free of them yet that doesn't put Lessie's life at risk."

Jallis shook his head. "You've both been through quite an ordeal," he said, looking quite guilty now. "I've felt terrible, watching Lessie suffer being chained up these past weeks, and for no good reason."

"Which is exactly why we didn't come back," I said flatly. "Because we knew we weren't going to receive fair treatment. Has Lord Tavarian made it back to the mainland?"

"If he has, I haven't heard of it yet."

I sighed. "Then there is no one to corroborate my version of events, which means I'll be found guilty. What's going to happen to me if you bring me back and I'm convicted?"

Jallis winced. "Normally, you would be executed if you were found guilty. But because you're a dragon rider, the worst they can do is give you life in prison. However," he added before I could protest, "if you can prove your innocence, you'll be fine. I convinced the colonel to allow me to try to get you to return voluntarily, and if you do, it would go a long way toward showing the court that you didn't actually desert."

I scowled. "I'm not sure that's going to matter to her."

"Come on, Zara," Jallis pleaded, desperation edging his voice. "Don't make yourself an enemy of the state. If you come back with me, I can tell the others your story, and they'll be forced to wait for Tavarian to return before they make any decisions. He is the head of your house, after all, and as a council member his word carries weight. We'll sort things out." He grasped my hand. "I know things have been rough between us, but I'm still your friend. I'll do whatever I can to help you."

Tears threatened the corners of my eyes at the warmth in Jallis's words, and I was tempted to wrap them around me like a comforting blanket. "What about Lessie?" I demanded instead. "Did she ever make it back to camp? She tried to come and retrieve me yesterday but almost got ambushed by the dragons tailing her."

"Not as far as I know," Jallis said, his expression growing dark again. "I know Lessie is acting out of loyalty to you, but the fact that she's flying around all alone during wartime is very dangerous for her. You owe it to her to come back to camp, where at least the two of you will be safe."

*Safe.* I was certain Lessie would argue whether being chained up at camp was truly "safe." "I was in more danger when I was sent out on patrol with incompetent superiors," I pointed out. And yet being a fugitive in wartime, hunted by both sides, would be terrible for both of us. "But fine," I said on a sigh. "I'll come back with you." A bad feeling twisted in my gut at the words, but what else could I do? I didn't want to stay here with Salcombe either, I reminded myself.

"Good." Jallis stood up and offered me a hand. "Let's go."

But before we could take more than two steps, a bevy of city guards entered the building, dressed in colorful historic uniforms and brass helmets. Salcombe walked straight toward them, his expression set in lines of grim determination.

"Mr. Trentiano," the lead guard, a lieutenant, greeted him brusquely. "Where is this troublemaker?"

Salcombe turned and pointed toward Jallis. "That man there is an Elantian officer," he said in strident tones. "I recognize him from my time in Zuar City. He has doubtless been sent here as a spy, here to cause mischief and throw Dardil's neutrality into question. You must arrest him immediately!"

Jallis stiffened, and I immediately clenched my hand around my weapon as they surrounded us, ready to fight if necessary. "Is this true?" the lieutenant demanded. "Where are your papers, and what is your business here?"

"My business?" Jallis asked, then flicked his hand through the air. A smoke bomb went off, filling the space with thick black smog. "Come on, Zara!" He grabbed my arm and shouldered his way through the officers, barreling toward the door.

But I wasn't nearly as nimble as Jallis, and I almost immediately tripped over my skirts. Jallis's fingers slipped through my hand as I tumbled to the ground, and a pair of strong arms squeezed around my midsection. "No!" I screamed, thrashing against the officer. I tried to go for my weapons, but the man held me too tightly, and my skirts got in the way yet again. I hated this blasted garment so much!

"I'm sorry, Zara!" Jallis yelled, his voice faint. I sagged against the guard's grip, knowing he was already beyond their reach, and therefore mine.

I was alone again.

Gradually, the smoke cleared from the lobby, restoring sight to everyone. The guard didn't release his grip on me, and I decided not to go for my weapons. Killing one of the guards would give me a one-way trip to the gallows, and there was no way I was getting out of here now, not with all these witnesses.

"You may unhand my wife," Salcombe said calmly, heading toward me. "She is not a spy, like the other."

"Are you certain?" the head guard asked, and the one holding me made no move to let go. "She seemed to be in league with him."

"My wife is...gullible," Salcombe said, his lip curling. "She was taken in by the young soldier's charms. But she is no spy, and as she is my wife, I would prefer to be allowed to deal with her disloyalty myself."

Rage filled me at Salcombe's condescending tone, so potent that I actually vibrated with it. The guard restraining me tightened his grip, but the head guard gave him a look that very clearly said *stay out of this*.

"Very well," he told Salcombe, then turned to the guard. "Let her go."

The city guard released me, and I made a break for the exit, pumping my arms and legs as fast as I could. I nearly made it to the doors before Salcombe appeared in front of me in a blur, far faster than any human could manage. He slapped his hand on my forearm, and I felt the prick of a needle. My brain immediately went fuzzy, and I glanced down to see the poison ring on his hand.

"I had a feeling you'd try something," he said, his voice distorted as my vision darkened around the edges. "So I came prepared."

The world slid sideways, and my enemy caught me right before I blacked out.

When I came to, I was back in the carriage, lying on my side on the bench. Groaning, I tried to lift my hands to my throbbing temple, but they were tied behind my back, the rope so tight that my hands had gone numb while I was out. Panic spiked in my blood, and my eyes flew open to find Trolbos sitting across from me. An ugly grin spread across his thuggish face as he saw I was awake.

"Finally come back to us now, have you, bitch?" he sneered. "I knew you couldn't be trusted. It was only a matter of time before you showed your true colors."

"Enough, Trolbos," Salcombe said, his voice like ice. "I am not pleased with you, either. Zara's escape attempt might have been successful if I hadn't stopped her at the door." The implication that Trolbos was at fault was crystal clear.

Trolbos set his jaw, his eyes blazing with hatred. "I'm sorry, sir. It won't happen again."

"No, it won't," Salcombe said softly. He'd never once turned to look at us, his eyes trained on the landscape. Night had fallen, and though the sky was still cloudy, it was clear enough to allow the moon to illuminate the fields rolling past us. Opening my senses, I immediately knew that we were nearing the estate. The heart's distinctive *gong* sounded in my head, tugging at my soul. The treasure hunter in me wanted to find it, wanted to dig it up and finally hold it in my hands. Despite coming within spitting distance of two different pieces, I'd never actually seen one in the flesh.

But the heart wasn't the only thing close by, I realized. Lessie was near too—only a few miles away. *"Zara,"* she said urgently. *"Are you all right? I've been trying to reach you!"*

*"Salcombe drugged me. I just woke up,"* I said, my mental voice groggy. Whatever sleeping serum he'd injected in me had packed quite the punch—part of me wanted to close my eyes again and drift into that deep, dark sleep. *"We're very close to a piece of the dragon god's heart, Lessie."* I sent her a mental image of the estate.

*"I'll meet you there,"* Lessie said. *"We'll take out Salcombe and his lackeys before they dig up the heart."*

Hope surged in my chest, but I didn't allow myself to be lulled into a false sense of security—there were all kinds of things that could go wrong. "This is foolish," I said to Salcombe, trying to appeal to his sense of reason. "We're breaking into an occupied estate. How are you going to get in, dig up the heart, and get out without being spotted? You can't hope to drug everyone into a stupor like you did when we broke into that townhouse in Zallabar."

"Stop asking questions," Salcombe ordered. "Your only

concern is to locate the heart. You are not in charge of the logistics."

"No, but I'll still be hanged if we're caught."

"And you'll be killed if you continue to refuse to cooperate." Rage distorted Salcombe's face as he gripped my chin hard enough to bruise. The madness had taken him fully, and my throat closed with fear. "Have I made myself clear?"

I spat in his face.

The resulting slap rattled my teeth, pain blooming on my cheek. Tears smarting, I collapsed back against the bench, real fear seeping into my bones. *"Hurry, Lessie,"* I called desperately, wriggling my hands against the rope as surreptitiously as I could manage. Trolbos had tied his knots very well, but if I kept at it, perhaps I could loosen them enough to get free.

*If only I could get to my knives,* I thought morosely. If I ever got out of this, I wasn't going to make this mistake again. I'd take a leaf from Trolbos's book and get knives I could hide in the toes of my boots or against the insides of my forearms.

The carriage rolled to a stop outside the estate, and this time, Salcombe had it drive right up to the gates. At first, I wondered how he'd managed to convince a driver to commit a burglary with him, but when Trolbos marched me out of the carriage, still tied up, I saw Hickam on the driver's bench. For a moment, I was afraid he'd come with us, and I'd have to contend with three men, but to my relief, he stayed behind.

"Not a sound," Salcombe warned as he picked the lock on the iron gates. There was a click as the bolt slid free, and Trolbos pushed it open easily, as if it weighed nothing. "If you try to alert anyone to our presence, I will have Trolbos kill them."

*Shit.* That had been next on my list of things—to scream at the top of my voice so the residents would come out and investigate. But aside from having superhuman strength, Salcombe and Trolbos were both very well trained. Trolbos had enough knives on him to take out five men before they were close enough to do any damage. If I thought alerting the house would actually stop Salcombe from digging up the heart, I would have done it, but there was no point in needlessly risking these poor people's lives.

"In any case," Salcombe said pleasantly as we walked through the open gate, as though we were merely going on a night time stroll, "we may get lucky and find that the piece of heart is in the grounds, which means there will be no need to go into the house. Zara, do you sense anything?"

I turned up the volume on my treasure sense, focusing on the heart. It was hidden beneath an old sundial in the gardens, around the back of the house. "I do sense it," I lied to Salcombe, "but the call is diffused, not easy to pinpoint. The mages who hid it must have sealed it in a box that is scrambling the location."

Salcombe scowled. "I do not believe you," he said, and signaled with his hand. Trolbos shifted, and I stilled at the feel of cold, sharp steel at my windpipe. "Try again, Zara."

Frantic, I scanned the grounds for a believable place that would stall Salcombe until Lessie could arrive. "T-try there," I stammered, jerking my head toward a small fish pond some distance from the house. "Beneath the water."

"If it is not there, I will order Trolbos to cut off your right hand," Salcombe said. He turned away, striding toward the pond.

Spikes of fear drove themselves into my heart as Trolbos marched toward the pond. In truth, there *was* something valuable buried in the pond—a large sapphire brooch—so I might be able to pass it off as a false alarm. But Salcombe was fully immersed in the dragon god's madness—he might cut off my hand anyway, just to make a point as he had with those guards.

The three of us waded into the water together, and I shivered as the cold liquid sluiced past my knees, nearly to my hips. "Well?" Salcombe demanded. "Anything?"

"Over here." I led them to the left, where I sensed the sapphire, and pointed with my nose. "Dig there."

Salcombe took my arm and Trolbos bent down, digging through the mud with his bare hands. His eyes widened in triumph as he came across something. "Found it!"

"Give it to me!" Salcombe ordered as Trolbos came up with a small, half-rotted wooden box. He released me to snatch it from him, and I immediately stepped back, out of range. *"Lessie?"* I called, my blood pounding in my ears. *"Where are you?"* She should have been here by now, but she still felt like she was at least a mile away.

*"Sorry,"* she said, and I could sense her stress and fear. *"I was almost there, but something didn't feel right, so I doubled back. I'm coming in now, from a different direction. Hang on, Zara!"*

I took another step back as Salcombe opened the box,

revealing the large sapphire brooch inside. Trolbos swore loudly, swinging around to face me. "You lied!" he roared.

"I didn't!" I cried, backpedaling out of the pond. The water had helped me loosen the ropes enough to slip my hands free, and I reached into my sodden skirts for my dragon blade. "I told you something was messing with my senses. Please, let me concentrate!"

"Quiet, both of you!" Salcombe snapped as a dog started barking, roused by our shouts. Trolbos immediately shut his mouth, and I backed toward the trees, hoping to melt into the darkness.

A door opened, and the dog's shrill barks grew louder as he raced toward our location. To my disappointment, he was a small beast, only a little larger than a house cat, and certainly no threat to either Salcombe or Trolbos.

"Sammie!" a childlike voice yelled, and my stomach dropped as a little boy, no more than six years old, rushed out of the house.

"Corbin, wait!" His mother was right behind him, along with a boy of fifteen, all still in their night clothes. The mother held a torch in one hand, the youth a sword, but both stopped short as Trolbos darted from the water, far faster than a man of his bulk had any right to move, and snatched up the child.

"Mama!" the boy wailed as Trolbos pressed a knife to his little throat.

"Stop right where you are and move no farther," Salcombe said in a soft, deadly voice. He glided from the water like a phantom, his cold gaze trained on me. In the background, the dog continued to bark, not even remotely intimidated by the threat. "And *you* will tell me where the piece of heart is, *now*. Or the boy will die."

"I won't tell you anything unless you let him go," I said stubbornly, but Trolbos dug the very tip of the knife in. The delight on Trolbos's face as a thin rivulet of blood spilled down the boy's chest was a monstrous thing to behold, and fear gripped my heart in a vise as the mother began to wail.

"No, no, not my Corbin!" She lunged for her child, but the older son held her back, his pale face twisted with both fury and terror. "Please, don't hurt my child!" The dog's barking grew even more ferocious, and he darted forward, nipping at Trolbos's heels. Without glancing down, Trolbos booted the animal with his foot, and the boy started crying in earnest as the dog landed hard at his mother's feet, whimpering in pain.

"All right, all right!" I shouted, unable to stomach the scene. I hated that I was giving in so easily, knowing what was at stake, but I couldn't let Trolbos kill that child. "The sundial. It's buried beneath the sundial in the back garden!"

Salcombe smiled. "Excellent." He turned to Trolbos. "The shovel, please."

Trolbos released the knife from the boy's neck to unhook the shovel on his back, then tossed it to Salcombe. The boy's mother whimpered when he replaced the knife with his hand instead, cradling the child's neck almost tenderly. A vicious wave of anger ripped through me at the terror on that family's face, and I would have drawn my dragon blade right then and there if not for the risk to the child's life.

"Stay back," Salcombe ordered the mother and her older son. To Trolbos and me, he said, "Come."

Trolbos released the child, who immediately ran toward his mother. The woman sobbed as she embraced him, and bundled her family back into the house as I reluctantly followed Trolbos and Salcombe to the back garden. The sundial sat in the center of a small clearing, a ray of moonlight sparkling on the stone surface.

"Show me exactly where," Salcombe ordered.

I found the spot, and Salcombe started digging. *"Lessie,"* I said urgently.

*"I know. Almost there."*

I'd hoped that Lessie would arrive before Salcombe managed to get very far, but his superhuman speed and strength allowed him to dig much faster than I'd anticipated. Within minutes, he'd cleared a four-foot hole. "Here we are," he said as his shovel struck against metal. "The moment of truth."

He ordered Trolbos to lift the box out of the hole. The box was pitch black, made of obsidian, with runes carved into the top and sides. Salcombe took the box from Trolbos and ran his hands over the surface, searching for a seam or latch or something with which to pry open the box, but there was nothing.

"Put it on the ground," Trolbos said. "I'll smash it open."

"No." Salcombe's eyes were bright as he traced the runes. "These protection runes are very powerful. They will obliterate you if you try to open the box by force. It would seem that we need a mage who can undo the spell and get to the heart within."

The terrible tightness in my chest eased somewhat—the Toppenfeld family had clearly taken precautions. Tavarian had also heavily spelled his own piece of heart, and I imagined all of them were similarly protected. How had Salcombe managed to get the piece he had? Did he have a mage on call who could break through these magical defenses?

*It doesn't matter,* I told myself. I had to get the box from Salcombe before he figured out how to open it. I lunged for Salcombe, my skirts in one hand and a knife in the other. My aim was true as I tossed the blade at his chest.

Salcombe moved like lightning, evading the throw easily. But my blade struck the box, and it flew from his grasp. I changed direction, barreling toward it, but Trolbos was there already, snatching it up in his meaty fist. I skidded to a halt, my skirts still in one hand as I drew my dragon blade with the other. The blades automatically extended to full width, and I spun the weapon in my hand as I oscillated between Trolbos and Salcombe as they both advanced on me, weapons drawn.

"I knew you would betray me eventually, Zara, but I'd hoped you'd wait a bit longer," Salcombe said. I'd expected him to be angry, and the mingled sadness and disappointment on his face took me by surprise. "I had hoped to convince you to remain by my side, to become one of my generals. The dragon god will need an army, and you and your Lessie would have been perfect additions."

I barked out a laugh. "If Lessie and I have learned anything, it's that military life doesn't suit us. Not Elantia's military, and certainly not the army of a depraved dragon whose sole aim is to bleed our world dry."

Salcombe's eyes blazed, and he lifted his weapon. "You have always been a small-minded fool—"

Lessie chose that moment to swoop in on near-silent wings,

her teeth flashing in the moonlight as she opened her terrifying maw. I jumped back right before she blasted both men with fire, but the rippling heat was so intense that I was certain every inch of my exposed skin looked like a boiled lobster. Salcombe and Trolbos both dodged the blast, but Lessie remained undeterred —she snatched up the hulking henchman in her jaws and dug her teeth into him with a crunch of bone that was both sickening and satisfying.

"The box!" I cried, arrowing toward it as it fell to the ground. But Salcombe was faster yet again, snatching it up with one hand while he parried my dragon blade with the other. The two of us traded furious blows, but I was no match for Salcombe's superhuman speed, especially with these stupid skirts tripping me up at every second. He dodged my whirling blades, then slammed the pommel of his blade into the side of my head. Pain exploded through my skull as I fell to the ground, and Lessie's roar of rage was the last thing I heard before I blacked out.

IT SEEMED like I was only unconscious for a few seconds, but when I woke up, I was in the sky. Strong arms cradled my midsection, and I breathed in as cold winds whipped around me. My head throbbed so badly I could hardly form a thought, and I swallowed as a wave of nausea rolled through me. Dragon's balls, what happened to me?

"Zara." Jallis's voice was low in my ear. "How are you feeling?"

Relief rushed through me at the familiar voice, but it was short-lived. I reached up to touch my injury, and the clank of chains chilled me to the bone. Opening my eyes, I turned my head—ignoring the excruciating pain that caused—and noted that we weren't alone. There were two other riders flanking us—lieutenants like Jallis, but older and more experienced. They briefly glanced my way, and the scorn in their cold gazes made my stomach churn.

"As well as any prisoner with a head injury," I said in a scathing tone, unsure who I was angrier with. Why did I think that Jallis had come to save me? Had I learned nothing?

Jallis sighed, pulling away. I squinted up at him, trying to see his expression, but my vision was blurry. "You know it has to be this way, Zara." He sounded genuinely sorry about it, and my anger wavered. Jallis might claim to be my friend, but his loyalty was to the military first, and he'd already told me that his mission was to bring me back. That hadn't changed just because my situation had shifted. "At least your injury will work in your favor. It's proof that you weren't in league with Salcombe."

"Like Colonel Roche gives a damn about that," I said, bitterness seeping into my tone. I reached through the bond for Lessie, and some of my anxiety abated as I sensed her flying directly behind us. "How did you find us?"

"Lessie, of course," Jallis said. "Bas and Jensen have been tracking her from a safe distance."

They must have been the danger Lessie had sensed. Another wave of fury hit me—if the dragons hadn't interfered, hadn't delayed Lessie's arrival, I might have been able to wrest the box from Salcombe. What happened to him, anyway? Had

Lessie managed to injure or kill him? I didn't sense the piece of heart anywhere nearby, so clearly the riders hadn't captured him or taken it off him.

"*Lessie, what happened while I was out?*" The bond told me that she was flying directly behind the rider on Jallis's left.

"*I attacked Salcombe and managed to injure his left arm,*" Lessie said. "*If not for the dragon god elixir, I would have taken him down, but even with the injury he was fast, and he made a run for it. I would have given chase, but Jallis and the others landed in the clearing and boxed you in. I had no choice but to come to your side.*"

"*You should have pursued him anyway,*" I argued, fury heating my blood. I hated that Salcombe was in the wind again, and that these dragon riders, the very people who were at risk if Salcombe succeeded in his quest to resurrect the dragon god, had foiled my attempt to subdue him. With Salcombe's resources, it was only a matter of time until he figured out how to open that second box.

"*Don't ask that of me,*" she snapped, on edge. "*We've only just been reunited, and you were unconscious and in danger on top of it all. Salcombe could have killed you with that strike, and I was worried that if I pursued him, I might come back to find you on death's door.*"

"*You're right. I'm sorry.*" I swallowed against the sudden lump in my throat and stroked the jagged edges of Lessie's mind through the bond. "*Thank you for saving me,*" I said. "*I don't know what I'd do without you.*"

Lessie sniffed. "*You'd better heal quickly,*" was all she said.

*"I've never had a headache before today, and I don't like it one bit."*

I swallowed down an unexpected urge to laugh. "You three took quite a risk, pursuing me into neutral territory," I said to Jallis. "Now that Zallabar has officially declared war, don't you think this is a waste of resources? What if Dardil's military had seen you and started shooting?"

"Luck was on our side, and we felt fairly comfortable taking the risk in the middle of the night." But Jallis's body tensed against mine. "Colonel Roche has a more...cavalier attitude than other officers when it comes to the use of dragon riders. It's something I've been meaning to write to General Sarte about."

I clenched my jaw. "And yet you have no problem following her orders anyway, despite her blatant disregard for dragon safety."

Jallis sighed. "She's one of those officers who has a chip on her shoulder because she was born a ground-dweller and had to fight for her position against dragon riders that have gotten promotions simply because of their pedigree," he said. "I don't entirely blame her for being frustrated, and though you're right that she shouldn't allow her prejudices to cloud her judgment, she's still our commanding officer. And she wouldn't have been promoted to her current position if she wasn't a good leader."

I had some choice words to say about our *good leader* but decided to refrain. The other dragon riders might not be able to hear me over the winds, but their mounts could, and I didn't need my comments getting back to Roche when my fate was still uncertain.

Tears of grief and frustration pricked at my eyes, and I

closed them, not wanting Jallis to see my weakness. Once, I would have turned my face into that solid, warm chest and found comfort in his strength, but I was no longer certain if I could trust him with my feelings.

*"It will be all right, Zara,"* Lessie said, trying to soothe me through the bond. *"As long as we're together, we're whole. We'll figure a way out of this."*

I nodded, trying to put on a brave face. But I was no longer so sure that was true.

ELEVEN

I expected to find the camp silent when we returned, but it was as busy as an anthill, soldiers swarming everywhere. Hardly anybody turned to look as we landed outside the stables—they were all busy clearing out buildings, loading up wagons, and doing other activities that looked suspiciously like we were moving.

"What's going on?" I asked Jallis.

"I'm not sure." Jallis frowned. "It's been nearly a week since I left camp."

We dismounted, and I had to clutch at Jallis's arm to stay upright, the pain and nausea making my legs shaky and weak. I wanted to give Lessie a hug, or at least touch her, but the two older dragons immediately herded her back to the stables before I could gather enough strength to walk over to her. To my relief, I didn't feel any anger or pain through the bond, which meant they weren't shackling or sedating her. They didn't have to anymore, now that they had me as a hostage to ensure her good behavior.

I, on the other hand, wasn't nearly so lucky.

"Lieutenant." Two large, burly soldiers stepped up, so close in features that I knew they had to be brothers, if not twins. "We've been ordered to escort Private Kenrook to the colonel's tent."

"I appreciate the assistance, but that won't be necessary," Jallis said, tightening his grip on my upper arm. "I can handle it myself."

"That's not your choice," the one on the left said. "The colonel said you wouldn't be needed."

A scowl briefly darkened Jallis's features before he smoothed it away. "Of course," he said tightly, handing me over to them. "I'm sorry, Zara," he said, quietly enough that only I would hear.

I gave him the barest of nods, then raised my chin and squared my shoulders as the soldiers marched me toward Colonel Roche's office. A few soldiers cast looks of disdain my way as we passed, but I didn't acknowledge them—I had nothing to be ashamed of. Lessie and I hadn't done anything wrong.

*"You are a hero."* Tavarian's voice echoed in my head. *"No matter what anyone else might say to you, I will always remember what you have done."*

The memory of that conversation—the last we'd had—both warmed my heart and chilled my blood. I hoped those words wouldn't be the last I'd heard from him. That he'd made it out alive.

"Colonel," the soldier gripping my left arm said as I was dragged before her desk. "The prisoner."

*The prisoner.* I barely managed to stop myself from snarling as Roche lifted her head. Her eyes briefly glinted with what I could only call smugness, but she barely acknowledged me before turning back to the papers on her desk. "Throw her in a cage."

"Wait!" I struggled against the soldiers' grips, but it was useless. The motion only increased the throbbing in my head, and my gorge surged into my throat as black spots flickered in my vision. "You're not even going to ask me for my side of the story? I spent nearly three weeks in Traggar! I have important information for you."

Roche looked up from her papers again and pinned me with a frigid stare. "Whatever information you may or may not have on Traggar is irrelevant," she said. "Now that Traggar has officially pulled out of the pending alliance with Zallabar, we have no need to worry about them. Zallabar, on the other hand, has launched an attack at the border, so we are deploying our troops to assist."

Terror spiked through me—Rhia and Ykos were at that border, likely fighting for their lives. "Let me go with them," I said desperately. "I can help."

Colonel Roche barked a laugh. "You will be—in a cage, where you will be held until your court-martial. Since we are at war, I have no idea when that will be. It could be in a week, or it could be a few months." This time she allowed the smugness to reach her mouth, her lips curving in a smile that made my chest grow tight. "The general will deal with you when he sees fit, and trust me when I say that he is a *very* busy man."

"This is insa—"

"Dismissed." She cut me off with the flick of a hand. "Take her away."

The soldiers hauled me out of the room and locked me in an open-air iron cage in the middle of the camp, leaving two lower-ranked soldiers behind to guard me. Despair filled me as I sank to the ground, resting my back on the cold bars as I sank my head into my hands. There was nowhere to go from here—my lockpicks and weapons had been taken from me while I was unconscious, and Lessie couldn't help me. Lifting my head, I scanned the camp for any sign of my fellow dragon riders from the academy, but there was none. It was likely they'd already been deployed.

*"Lessie?"*

*"I'm here,"* she said, and I felt a surge of anger from her. *"I listened to the conversation between you and Roche. What a despicable woman."*

I sighed. *"Can you tell Kadryn I want to talk to Jallis?"*

A pang of sadness. *"He is gone,"* she said. *"Almost immediately after you were taken away, Jallis was given orders to deploy. Only eight dragons remain, not including me."*

I started to ask if Lessie had gleaned any more information from her fellow riders, but the pain in my head suddenly intensified, and my vision began to blur again. "Shit," I groaned aloud, cradling my head in my hands.

*"Zara?"* Lessie's urgent voice was like a hot spike driven straight through my skull. *"Zara, are you all right?"*

"It hurts," I moaned, tears trickling out of the corners of my eyes. The back of my head throbbed so badly it felt like someone was repeatedly smashing a hammer into my skull. "Private," I croaked aloud, trying to get the attention of my guard. "I need medical attention."

The private turned to look at me, his eyes narrowed in suspicion. "You're just trying to get me to let you out of your cage."

Another crippling wave of pain seized me, so intense I flopped sideways onto the metal floor. Nausea cramped my gut, and I closed my eyes, trying to escape the pain.

An ear-splitting roar shook the air, worsening my headache. Shouts filled the air, and then the ground rumbled as Lessie raced into the camp, knocking aside soldiers in her haste to reach me. I opened my eyes and gasped at the sight of deep gouges on her shoulder, large enough that they could only have come from a dragon's claw. Indeed, there was a larger dragon on her heels, but Lessie evaded him. She skidded to a halt in front of my cage and turned her blazing eyes on my guard, roaring at him so loudly that the very earth shook. The guard looked like he was going to piss himself, racing around the other side of the cage to put distance between him and Lessie.

"What does she want?" he wailed, brandishing his sword. "Why is she attacking me?"

"She's not," a man, one of the dragon riders who escorted me back to camp with Jallis, said. He locked gazes with me, and I was surprised to see a flicker of sympathy in his deep blue eyes. "She's just angry because her rider isn't receiving medical attention. Kenrook took a nasty blow to the head before we retrieved her."

"I thought she was lying about the injury," the guard grumbled.

"What is the meaning of this?" Colonel Roche shouted, striding into the clearing. Her eyes nearly bulged out of her skull at the sight of Lessie, bleeding and angry as she crouched outside my cage. The dragon who'd chased after her waited at a safe distance, as if he were ready to pounce on Lessie if she made a wrong move. Despite my addled brain, I wondered if the scratches on Lessie's shoulder were just for show—the other dragon was much larger and, along with the others, could have easily subdued her. It was almost as if they sympathized with Lessie and were trying to help her defend me.

"Kenrook's dragon escaped the enclosure to come to the aid of her rider," the other rider said. "She has a concussion and requires urgent medical attention."

"She's a prisoner," Roche started to say, but was cut off by another roar from Lessie. Her face went white when tendrils of smoke curled from my dragon's nostrils. I'd never seen Lessie quite so angry before. I had a feeling that if Colonel Roche had been anyone else, my dragon would have already severed her thick head from her stubborn shoulders.

"Ma'am," the other rider began, hesitant.

"Get the healer," she snapped. "If she's still on the base. Can't have her dying before the court-martial date, can we?" She gave me an ugly smile. "The moment she's patched up, load up the cage. We're moving out."

Lessie stayed by my side while we waited for the healer—a female mage who looked to be older than time itself—to arrive. She stayed by my side while the healer cradled my head through the bars, using her magic to repair the head wound and undo whatever damage my brain had suffered. The pain gradually receded, and the moment she lifted her hands from my head, I sat up.

"I've managed to repair the damage," the healer said stiffly. "Though I should have been called sooner. A few minutes more and you would have suffered permanent brain damage."

"Thank you for healing me," I said fervently, and looked around for that other dragon rider so I could thank him, too. But he was already gone, though his dragon had been left behind to guard Lessie. Briefly, I wondered if he'd helped me because of Roche's dismissive treatment—she hadn't even wanted to see Jallis or the other riders who'd brought me back, who should have been commended for executing a swift, painless retrieval. Somehow, the thought that at least she was equally prejudiced against all riders made me feel somewhat better about the whole situation.

But those feelings were short-lived when the rider returned, and two other dragons landed in the clearing. "Colonel Roche has ordered us to escort your dragon to the border," he said, striding over to his own dragon. He dumped an armful of tack on the ground and began to saddle him up. "You'll be transported by wagon."

"By wagon?" I asked aloud as Lessie snarled. "Why? One of you could easily tie me to your saddles."

The rider gave me a grim smile. "Colonel Roche isn't going to allow you any privileges, and that includes the privilege of flying, even if it is on another dragon's back. You'll just have to slum it on the ground with the other soldiers until you make it to the new base."

Some of the other soldiers nearby shot the rider dirty looks, but he didn't even spare them a glance as he mounted. *"Go with him,"* I said to Lessie, knowing that she was preparing to dig her heels in.

She gave me an incredulous look. *"I'm not leaving you."*

*"You're not. We're going in the same direction. You're just going to be a little...ahead of me."* I gave her a lopsided smile, trying to alleviate the tension. But Lessie wasn't in the mood— she snarled at the other three dragons as they herded her back into the field, preparing to take flight.

*"GO,"* I said, infusing the word with a command. Lessie couldn't disobey a direct order, so she took flight, screeching her protests even as she flapped her wings. Tears burned in my throat as I watched her soar through the sky with the other dragons. I wished so badly to be up there with her, but I reminded myself that we weren't being separated. I'd see her in a few days.

*At least you won't have to worry about Salcombe finding you,* I thought sourly, but that was of little comfort. In fact, I almost wished the bastard had one of my hairs, so I could take the piece of heart back from him when he came to find me again. The fact that the war had started would only work in Salcombe's favor—while Elantia and its neighbors were distracted, he would slip between the borders and finish the dragon god's work. And once he did, the war between Elantia and Zallabar would look like child's play.

A s promised, my cage was loaded up onto the back of
a wagon, packed in with heavy bags of grain so it
would not slide around. Even so, the journey was
extremely uncomfortable—the wagon, one in a long line of
similar conveyances making up the caravan, moved incredibly
slow, even by human standards, and the road was harsh and full
of potholes. Each jostle had some part of my body banging
against the unforgiving metal bars. Even curling up into the
fetal position didn't help. The only good thing about this situation was that the soldiers had given me a military uniform to
change back into, but that did nothing to cushion me from the
cage. My back would be one giant mess of bruises by the time
we arrived at the border.

*I wonder if I'll get to see Rhia,* I thought morosely as I stared
up at the twinkling stars that were the only bright spot of this
miserable night. I wasn't certain how I felt about the idea. On
the one hand, I desperately needed a friend, but on the other

hand, Rhia wouldn't be able to do anything to help me. She wasn't as rigid in her loyalty to the military as Jallis, but as a low-ranking rider, she had no power. I wasn't about to ask her to break any of the rules—unlike Jallis, she was from a minor house, and wouldn't be offered the same level of leniency.

*If only I could get to my lockpicks, I could be free of this place already,* I grumbled to myself, glancing to the driver. My belongings were in a pack that sat on the driver's bench, bouncing with every pothole we hit. I was terrified that it would bounce straight out of the wagon and onto the road where the endless parade of wheels would crush it. Almost everything within was a priceless, one-of-a-kind item, and the dragon blade was the only link to my parentage. I couldn't bear the thought of losing any of it.

I was just starting to drift off when emotions from Lessie surged inside me. *"Get ready, Zara!"*

I bolted upright, startled by the urgency in her voice. *"What are you doing?"* I asked.

A few minutes later, I got my answer as Lessie dove through a thick layer of clouds, barreling straight toward the wagon. Several of the horses, including the ones pulling my wagon, immediately spooked, breaking away from the caravan and running onto the fields. Angry shouts and fearful screams filled the quiet night, but Lessie ignored the other wagons and headed straight for me. Sensing her intent, I gripped the bars as tight as I could as she swooped low, catching my cage in her talons and carrying it away from the wagon.

"Oi!" my driver shouted, his voice a mix of panic and anger. "Bring that back, you!"

Lessie deposited me a few feet away, then turned back to the cart. The driver's face went white with fear, and he snapped his reins, trying to outrun Lessie. But Lessie was far too fast, and with a swipe of her claws, she separated the horses from the wagon, bringing it to a halt.

"I think she wants you to free me," I drawled as Lessie snatched up the terrified soldier in her claws.

"All right!" he tried to shout, but it came out more like a squeal. Lessie put him down in front of my cage, and he immediately dug out the key from his pocket. "You crazy bitch," he said as he unlocked the cage, voice and hands shaking. The older soldiers maintained a healthy distance, unwilling to face Lessie's wrath. They knew she could torch them all in an instant if she wanted.

The gate swung open, but I didn't move. "Back up," I ordered, eyeing his weapons. The last thing I needed was to walk out only for him to run me through with his sword.

The man hesitated, but Lessie made the choice for him, putting her big body between us as she nudged him away. She'd gone back to the wagon to get my belongings, and I nearly cried in relief as she handed over the pack. Quickly, I unwrapped it and strapped my gear on. The feel of my weapons strapped onto my body without the trappings of a dress felt amazing, and for the first time, I could actually taste the beginnings of freedom.

*"Get on!"*

"Private!" the sergeant in charge of the caravan shouted as I leapt onto Lessie's back. His eyes glittered with fury as he trotted toward us on a horse, and his sword was drawn even though he had to know it was useless in the face of Lessie's armor. "Control your dragon at once and return to your cage!"

I laughed. "Do you really think I'm going to listen to you after the treatment I've suffered?"

"You're a prisoner," he snapped, "but you haven't yet been convicted, and there's a chance you could be cleared. If you leave now there is no going back, Private. You will be guilty of mutiny, and your bloody dragon rider privileges won't be able to save you," he added with a sneer.

I gritted my teeth, reminded that Colonel Roche wasn't the only one who was prejudiced against dragon riders. There was a very good chance that my hearing would be presided over by similarly prejudiced officers, and if Tavarian didn't make it back, I could very well be sentenced to death.

"Maybe I am a mutineer," I said to the soldier, aware that I was about to burn all my bridges with the military, "but I've done everything I could to serve and protect this country, and in return I've gotten nothing but hate. Tell Colonel Roche whatever you want about me. I have no faith in Elantian military justice, and I'm not going to let you punish me for doing what's right."

"Fly," I said to Lessie, squeezing her sides with my legs. I gripped the large spike near the base of her neck as she launched us into the air with a powerful beat of her wings. The soldier shouted something, but we ignored him, and my worries fell away as we shot into the sky, left on the ground along with my captors. Grinning, I tilted my head back and allowed the wind to whip my hair off my shoulders. We did it! We might be fugitives now, doomed to live as outlaws for the rest of our lives, but at least we were finally free.

"*You managed to slip your escort again?*" I asked Lessie, leaning into her hide so I could soak in her warmth. Without proper riding gear, the icy air would chill me to the bone if I didn't stick close to her skin.

"*Yes,*" she said, sounding quite smug about it. "*All of this night flying we've been doing has really come in handy, and unlike the other dragons, I wasn't carrying a load. Between their cargo and their riders, they were slowed considerably.*"

"*They'll still be chasing us, though,*" I said, my elation wearing off as worries settled on my shoulders once more. "*We need to find somewhere to lie low for a bit.*"

"*Agreed,*" Lessie said, though she sounded mournful about it.

We flew on for another twenty minutes or so, putting considerable distance between us and the caravan while we searched for a good place. Finally, we found a secluded valley populated by tall trees with thick foliage. Lessie managed to find a space large enough for us to land but still shaded enough that we would be difficult to spot from the sky.

The moment she touched the ground, I leaped off her back, my weapon drawn. Using our combined senses, we checked for any signs of human or dragon life in the area and found none. My treasure sense picked up a few valuables buried in the ground, but nothing that spoke of living humans nearby, and Lessie didn't scent anything other than wildlife.

Satisfied, I secured my blade, then threw my arms around Lessie's neck for a long, hard hug.

"*Thank you for coming back for me,*" I said fervently. Lessie wrapped one of her arms around me, squeezing me tightly against her as she rumbled a purr. Perhaps her grip was a bit too hard, but in this moment, I didn't care. She could squeeze me like this for the rest of my life as long as it meant we wouldn't be separated. "*I wish there had been another way, though. I hate that you keep putting yourself at risk like this. If it were just me defying them it would be one thing, but the military isn't going to tolerate an unruly dragon. They may execute both of us if we're recaptured.*"

"*Then we'll have to make sure that doesn't happen,*" Lessie said stubbornly. "*I don't regret breaking you out, Zara, not one bit. The other dragons told me that if you were convicted, you would be sent to a prison that's very far away for several decades. I am not going to live like that, especially when we haven't done anything wrong.*"

The thought of being locked away for the rest of my life, without being allowed to see or even communicate with my dragon, made my chest ache, and I hugged Lessie even harder. "*You're right,*" I said fiercely. Better to live free and happy for a short time than live a long but miserable life in a cage.

Lessie rumbled in agreement. "*Promise me that you won't leave me again,*" she said. "*No matter what happens, we won't be separated.*"

"*I promise,*" I said without reservation.

Lessie and I would have happily snuggled for a while longer, but hunger got the best of us—I hadn't eaten for at least a day, and the small meal Lessie had been fed when she'd been brought back to the stables had long worn off. Lessie took flight while I kept watch at our little campsite, and she came back a little while later with a large buck. She set her catch down and tore off a leg for me, then tucked into the animal with relish while I prepared my portion to cook.

"*So, what now?*" Lessie asked as I finished wrapping the skinned leg in thick leaves so Lessie could cook it with her flame. We didn't dare risk a proper fire—any dragons looking for us would be able to spot it from miles away—but we reasoned that a few minutes of Lessie's flame was worth the risk.

"*We need to go after Salcombe,*" I said, stepping back so Lessie could take over. She opened her maw and shot a thin stream of fire over the dressed leg.meat. With any luck, the leaves would allow the flame to cook the meat through without actually catching fire. "*We haven't been gone very long, and Salcombe is on his own—I bet he's still in Dardil.*"

"*Do you not think we should wait for Lord Tavarian to turn up?*" Lessie asked. "*Perhaps we can seek him out directly.*"

"*He said he would head straight to the camp when he was done in Traggar,*" I reminded Lessie. "*He hadn't turned up by the time we left, so that means he's likely still there, and we can't fly over Traggar without risking war. We also can't afford to go back to the camp and wait.*" Two pairs of dragon riders had remained, along with a contingent of soldiers, on the off-chance that Traggar decided to attack us anyway.

"*We could go to his island,*" Lessie suggested.

"*We'd have to find it first,*" I pointed out. Tavarian's floating island was in constant motion, and though I imagined he had a way of tracking it, I didn't. I didn't even know if it always followed the same trajectory—the only thing I knew was that the islands coasted on magnetic currents that pulled them through the air.

*"It has to operate on some kind of orbit,"* Lessie pointed out, *"as well as the other floating islands, or they would inevitably end up crashing into each other."*

*"Good point."* I briefly considered the idea—we could go to the floating island, or to the hidden valley, and try to get a message to Tavarian via his servants. But who knew how long we would end up waiting there? *"We can't afford to hang around,"* I said. *"The more time we waste looking for Tavarian, the more time Salcombe has to find the fourth piece."*

Lessie nodded. *"It's too late to hunt for him now,"* she said, looking up at the night sky. *"By the time we get to Dardil, dawn will have arrived. But we can lie low until nightfall and pursue him then. You should be able to locate him easily with your treasure sense."*

Decided, the two of us took to the skies again, somewhat rejuvenated by the brief rest and the food. It took us several hours, but we managed to make it past the Dardil border just as the first hints of twilight began to paint the sky. We landed in a thickly wooded forest. Lessie and I spent the rest of the day sleeping, each taking turns watching out for any intruders while we recovered our strength.

By the time dusk settled over the sky, we were both awake and anxious to get going.

*"Let's head east, toward the capital,"* I said once we were in the sky again. We were near Lange when Salcombe had escaped with the heart, and I had a feeling he'd be headed toward Zallabar, where he could use those false citizenship papers of

his to lie low. The Zallabarian border was only a few hours east of Lange, the low, flat land making for easy travel, and I wanted to catch him before he crossed into enemy territory.

We flew in companionable silence, staying above the clouds and out of sight. The cloud cover was thinner than usual, but I wasn't worried about being spotted at night. I kept my treasure sense wide open as we traveled, tuned to high-value objects, and my instincts itched as we passed over several large collections of treasure that were likely either hoards or the contents of hidden temples yet to be discovered. A few of my treasure hunting acquaintances had been to Dardil on digs and uncovered some valuable pieces—at any other time, I would have been tempted to stop and see if I could pick up anything to take back to the Treasure Trove for Carina to sell.

The thought of my shop made my heart ache with homesickness. I hoped that Carina and the orphans were all right. Now that Zallabar had officially declared war, the city's residents would be on alert, hoarding their supplies and spending less money than usual. Buying art and artifacts would take a back seat, even for the elite, which meant the shop would take a hit. Of course, we had plenty of money tucked away with all the good months we'd had, but that wouldn't help the employees who relied on us for steady work. Hopefully, Carina could find other ways to keep them busy so they wouldn't end up on the streets again.

"Zara." Lessie's urgent voice pierced my thoughts. "*Down below.*"

I leaned to the side to see that the clouds had parted, giving us an unobstructed view of the flatlands. At first, I wasn't certain what I was seeing—the ground looked like a giant chess-board, full of dark and light fields...except that unlike a chess-board, the fields were moving. My heart leapt into my throat as I realized I was staring down at an army.

*"Get closer,"* I ordered, and Lessie put on a burst of speed. We remained above the cloud layer, and I fastened my goggles over my eyes, using the dials to zoom in. My blood iced over as I surveyed the army—there were roughly seventy units of eight hundred out there, marching in formation, all wearing Zallabarian uniforms. A quarter of them were cavalry, and in addition to the men, they had countless armored vehicles—the horseless kind, I realized with horror, noting the clouds of steam puffing from the hoods. I'd seen prototypes of horseless carriages before, but I hadn't realized that the military would be using them, or building them to such size. The carriages were hauling large wagons full of the new cannons, and a quick count told me they had upwards of a thousand weapons. Overall, there had to be at least fifty thousand soldiers out there.

All moving west, toward Lange and the Elantian border.

"Fuck," I swore out loud. Those steam-driven vehicles headed straight for Lange, but it didn't take a genius to figure out that the Dardilian capital wasn't the main target. The Zallabarians likely planned to roll straight through the capital, and with the might of all those men and cannons, the city would likely surrender without much of a fight. From there, the troops would strike through into the unprotected north of Elantia, from where our own soldiers and dragons had just been called away.

*"The attack on the south,"* Lessie said in a voice that was somewhere between awe and terror. *"It must be a feint."*

*"Damn right, it's a feint,"* I growled, ordering her to fly higher into the clouds, far out of the range of those deadly cannons. *"That, or it's a genuine attack with a second army, and they plan on taking the country in a pincer maneuver. Either way, we've only got a handful of troops left behind to defend the capital against these bastards."* Not that we would have been able to do very much anyway—we'd had half that number stationed at the channel, and those cannons would have decimated us.

*"What do we do?"* Lessie asked. *"Should we keep looking for Salcombe?"*

I swore viciously. Once again, this stupid war was interfering with my real objective. But could I afford to turn away?? By tomorrow, Lange would be firmly under Zallabarian control, and under his guise as a Warosian businessman, Salcombe would likely be able to grease the right palms and slip away. In the meantime, Lessie and I were in greater danger than ever. We couldn't keep striking west toward Zallabar, not when this army was out in full force. For all I knew this was only the first wave, and Zallabar was sending even more troops.

*"We need to head back to the capital,"* I told Lessie. We'd already passed Lange and had moved on since we hadn't sensed the relic there. Normally, if I'd still been part of the army, I would have flown straight back to high command to warn them of the flanking attack so that they would not be completely taken by surprise. But as things stood right now, would they even believe me? And what *could* we do, with the timing and distance involved? From what I was able to glean, the bulk of the Elantian troops were massed along the mountainous

western border, far to the south of here. I didn't know if we'd be able to get there in time to make a difference—Lessie was much stronger than she'd been when she'd flown for the first time, but she was still young and tired easily, and we'd already done quite a bit of flying today.

No, the only thing we could do now was go to Lange and hope the people of Dardil were prepared to defend their neutrality against the might of a Zallabarian army.

THIRTEEN

Pushing hard, Lessie and I made it back to Lange well ahead of the enemy. The first of the cavalry would be hitting the town in the next two hours, so I had Lessie drop me atop a rampart. I'd overheard a staff member at the inn informing tourists that this rampart had been part of a large city wall that had formed the entire perimeter of the town—a wall that would have served Dardil quite well if the citizens, in their complacency, hadn't decided to tear it down.

The rampart reminded me of Zuar City's own walls. While they still stood, they hadn't been properly manned or maintained in centuries. If Zallabar made it through—and they would—they would head straight for my hometown. Still, perhaps Zuar City could be saved, or at least the damages could be minimized if the residents had sufficient warning.

Swinging down from the ramparts, I headed into Lange, striking out for the nearest guardhouse. On my way in, I passed by the inn where Salcombe and I had stayed, and I hesitated.

Salcombe wasn't there anymore, but it was likely he'd stopped by to collect his belongings on his way out. Perhaps he'd left some clue as to where he'd gone. Surely I could take a minute to find out; after all, if it turned out he hadn't gone to Zallabar, I could still pursue him.

Ignoring a stab of guilt, I pushed through the doors and headed to the front desk. To my surprise, the owner, a tall man in a suit with silver-blond hair and a thin face, was manning the reception.

"Mrs. Trentiano?" he asked, his pale eyes widening as he recognized me. "What—where—"

I hid a wince as he sputtered. No doubt he recognized me by my hair, and the sight of me wearing an Elantian military uniform threw him for a loop. "Yes, Mr. Desmet, it's me, but my name isn't really Trentiano," I said with an apologetic smile. "The man who was posing as my husband was actually my captor. I've managed to escape and have returned, hoping he left some of my belongings here."

"I'm afraid I can't help you with that," the owner said gruffly. "Mr. Trentiano checked out early this morning. I was surprised to see him here without you or that bodyguard of his, but I'm a discreet fellow and do not ask too many questions of my patrons." His cheeks colored as he likely realized he was being the opposite of discreet by telling me. "How do I know you are being truthful about your relationship to Mr. Trentiano?"

I gestured to my uniform. "I wasn't lying when I said that I am an Elantian soldier," I said, recalling that he'd been in the lobby when the city guard had descended on me and Jallis. "Trentiano is wanted for crimes in his home country."

The man's face cleared. "That explains why the city guard came looking for him," he said. "His carriage left toward the city harbor. No doubt he has taken berth on some vessel flying under a neutral flag, which would be safest in these troubled times." His brow furrowed. "It isn't easy being sandwiched between two countries at war, you know. I wonder how long the warring parties will continue to respect our neutrality."

"Not long at all, I'm afraid," I said, bringing my attention back to the immediate threat. I could go down to the docks and question the workers about where Salcombe had headed, but I doubted I would get much salient information, and we were running out of time. "On my way back to the city, I passed a large army heading here from the Zallabarian border. They should be arriving here in the next hour or two, so I'd suggest you secure your family while there is still time."

The man's face blanched. "An army?" he asked, gripping the edges of the counter. "How can you be sure?"

"I saw them with my own eyes," I insisted, refusing to tell him the truth—that I'd flown directly over them. "Fifty thousand strong, with armored horseless vehicles and at least a thousand of their new cannons. You can believe me or not—either way you'll be seeing them for yourself soon enough."

"Blast," he swore. He pulled on a bell rope hanging near the counter, then hurried out from behind it. "I must alert the city council at once."

I grabbed his arm. "Does the city have a contingency plan in place?"

"Of course," he said, somewhat impatiently. "I am part of the council and a few of us have considered the possibility that Zallabar might eventually go through us to get to Elantia. We hoped that this was just paranoia, but it seems that our unfortunate prediction has come to pass after all." He scowled at me, as if this whole situation were my fault, but then his face cleared. "Thank you for the timely warning," he said, shaking off my grip. "I must attend to my city now."

The rush of footsteps caught my attention, and several staff members poured into the lobby, bleary eyed and still in sleep attire. Desmet quickly briefed them of the situation, then sent them off to help warn his colleagues and get the wheels in motion. While the staff rushed about, I darted upstairs and search the rooms Salcombe had rented. I was able to get into them easily enough with my lockpick, but to my disappointment he'd left nothing behind, not even the extensive wardrobe he'd purchased for me. What did he think he was going to do with all those dresses and jewels? Try to sell them back to recoup some of his investment? Or was he keeping them in the hopes he could recapture me?

*More likely he didn't want to leave any traces behind,* I thought, shaking my head as I hurried down the stairs. With the way things had ended between us, I doubted Salcombe intended to take me alive. If the two of us met again, there would be no cooperation. It was kill or be killed now. In fact, Salcombe might already assume I was dead—if the healer hadn't fixed me, I would have died from that head wound by now.

The thought of having to drive my dragon blade into Salcombe's heart chilled me to the bone, but the sound of a loud bell gong distracted me. I rushed outside and stopped short at the sight of people rushing around in the dead of night, many of them half-dressed or still wearing nightclothes. Carts and horses were being harnessed, wailing children dragged out of their homes by harried mothers, and nearly every man carried a weapon of some kind. In the distance, a man tugged mightily on a large bell perched at the top of a tower, waking the citizens. City guards directed the flow of traffic, but it was still mayhem, and I immediately climbed to the roofs to avoid being trampled as I headed for the docks.

The marina also swarmed with activity, but since the city was just being roused, it hadn't turned into a madhouse yet. I swung down from the top of a building that sold fishing supplies and hurried over to one of the guards. He clenched his sword at the sight of me in my military uniform, and I held up my hands, stopping at a safe distance.

"I'm not here to cause any harm," I said, staying in the light so he could see I had no weapons in my hands. "I'm looking for an Elantian fugitive who may have come through here this morning. Have you seen him?" I gave him Salcombe's description. "He would be traveling alone, but with enough luggage for three or four people."

The man frowned thoughtfully. "I did notice a man like that —he was here quite early. I remember him because my captain came here asking after him." His expression darkened. "I'm not surprised to hear he's a fugitive—apparently he terrorized a family last night trying to burgle them, and killed one of his own men and left him to die on their property."

*They'd found Trolbos,* I thought, and a vicious sense of satisfaction swept through me as I remembered he was dead. "Do you have any idea where he's headed now?"

The guard shrugged. "He boarded a ferry headed east that stops at several islands in the northern sea—" he said, then was cut off by the sound of cannon fire, disturbingly close. He drew his sword, and I instinctively grabbed for my dragon blade as fear gripped my throat. Was the army already here? Who were they shooting at? The thought of one of those shrapnel bombs shredding Lessie's wings made my skin grow clammy, and I bolted from the docks, ignoring the shouted questions of the guard behind me.

*"Lessie!"* I cried, reaching for her through the bond. She didn't seem to be in any pain, though I could feel both excitement and fear quickening her blood. *"Where are you?"*

*"Coming your way now,"* she said as I burst onto a street. *"Get to a roof!"*

I scrambled up the first building I could find, then jumped straight onto Lessie's back as she swooped in low. Cries of alarm and terror floated up from the street as the Dardilians spotted her, but we ignored them as we shot skyward, Lessie pumping her wings to gain altitude as fast as she could. As we rose, I spotted the first columns of the approaching army, already mowing down the few guards standing in their way. A few cannons swiveled in their direction, and light flashed as they were set off.

*"Higher!"* I yelled, though I knew Lessie was flying as fast as she could manage. Two of the bombs flew low, but one of them exploded right beneath us. Lessie roared as one of the shrapnel bits nicked her wing. Luckily, we cleared the rest of it. Trem-

bling with shock at the near miss, we swerved west, away from the approaching army and back to the Traggaran channel and our old camp.

The Elantian army may have tried to imprison us, but there was no time to dwell on bad blood now. We needed to warn our fellow dragon riders of the approaching cannons before it was too late.

FOURTEEN

L essie and I barely made it over the Elantian border before she started to flag, exhausted after days of long, arduous flights. We pushed as long as we could, making it back to the coastline before she finally landed in a near collapse, her entire body trembling from exhaustion.

"It's all right," I soothed, stroking her wings as she lay down in the sand. We were still miles and miles from the camp, completely exposed on the beach with no cover in sight. "We'll rest for an hour and then move somewhere that's better protected so you can fully recover."

"We don't have time for that," Lessie said, her voice weary. "The Zallabarians will only need a fraction of that force to mow through the city. The rest of them will keep moving, and those armies are fresh and rested. If we stop for too long, we will be too late."

I gritted my teeth in frustration. The bone-deep weariness I sensed in Lessie alarmed me—how long could she keep this up before she injured herself? Now that those cannons were in play, Lessie would have to be at her best in order to avoid getting her wings torn apart by shrapnel. But that was even more of an impetus to head south—the last thing we needed was for the Zallabarian army to run into us. They would be only too happy to cut both of us to pieces.

Lessie rested on the ground for a solid hour, then flew low over the water and caught several large fish. She wolfed them down with relish, then brought back a sea bass for me, which I devoured after she charred it. The food seemed to invigorate her somewhat, and despite my misgivings, we were soon flying again.

On our way to the camp, we stopped at every town and village, partially to give Lessie short breaks, and partially to warn the guards of the impending attack. I answered questions about the approaching army while deflecting the ones about myself and how I'd come by the information, hoping they would look to my dragon for reassurance that I was a rider and knew what I was talking about. Luckily, the guards didn't seem overly suspicious of me, and my warnings deflected any undue interest.

Finally, after several hours of stop-and-go flight, we reached the camp. Lessie and I circled it from a safe distance, trying to decide what to do. As expected, the camp was almost completely empty, not a single dragon around. Lessie couldn't even sense any in the stables, which meant those riders were likely out on patrol. That boded well for us, as it meant there was no one strong enough to restrain Lessie when we landed.

But before I could give Lessie the order to descend, a jolt of excitement barreled through the bond. *"Look, Zara!"* she cried, and I peered through the clouds to see the shapes of two young dragons flying toward us. *"It's Rhia and Ykos!"*

"Do you know who she is with?" I asked, a thrill ripping through the grimness that had settled in my mind.

*"I don't recognize the dragon, but I imagine he is from the other border camp,"* Lessie said.

Lessie put on a burst of speed, and we intercepted the two dragons, who looked like they were approaching the camp as well. "Zara!" Rhia cried out, her eyes widening in mingled delight and relief. She wore full armor, her chestnut hair pulled back into a knot, though several strands had wormed their way free. There was a flush in her apple cheeks, and she flashed sparkling white teeth as she grinned. "You're alive!"

"This your treasure hunter friend?" the other dragon rider asked. He was older, in his early forties, with black-brown hair and a swarthy complexion. He scanned me curiously, and I was relieved to see no censure in his dark eyes. Maybe he hadn't heard about my court-martial.

"Treasure hunter *and* dragon rider," Rhia corrected him primly. "Why are you here, Zara? I thought you'd be heading for the other camp!"

The three of us landed so we could have a short discussion a safe distance from the camp. Rhia and I dismounted and ran to each other, and I threw my arms around her in a fierce hug. "I was so worried I wouldn't see you again when I heard you'd been stranded in Traggar," Rhia said into my ear, her voice choked with emotion. "They said you were a traitor, but I knew that couldn't be true and that something terrible must have happened. Please, tell me what's going on."

Sitting in the grass, with our dragons forming a protective circle, I told Rhia and her partner everything. As it turned out, the two of them had been sent here from the frontline in exchange for the dragon riders that had been moved farther south, including Jallis—it was clear that they were being side-lined, sent away from the worst fighting to protect their younger dragons. The irony did not escape me that if Lessie and I hadn't been branded as traitors, we likely would have been left behind as well, but due to my background as a thief and a treasure hunter, Roche hadn't trusted me enough to leave me behind in a sparsely manned camp that would be easier to escape from.

By the time I finished bringing Rhia up to speed on everything up to my re-capture by the Elantian army, she was shaking her head, incensed. "I can't stand officers like Roche," she said, her eyes flashing. "Just because she's been treated poorly in the past doesn't mean she should be taking it out on every dragon rider. In fact, I would think she would sympathize with you more, since you grew up as a ground-dweller!"

I shook my head. "The fact that I went from ground-dweller to dragon rider would only make her hate me more, since I've managed to accomplish something she never will."

"You still haven't explained what you're doing here," Nash, the other rider, said. "If you're a prisoner, why are you flying around free, and by yourself? I'm assuming you escaped?"

I nodded. "Lessie broke me free, and the two of us flew to Dardil in search of Salcombe." I didn't bother to explain who he was—there wasn't time. "Rhia, there was an army fifty thousand strong headed straight for Lange, with armored, steam-powered vehicles and nearly a thousand cannons." My blood went cold as I recalled the sheer enormity of the force. "They were on Lange's doorstep when I arrived, and have no doubt taken the city by now. I am certain their plan is to march straight through the country and strike Elantia from the north."

Rhia and Nash both went bone-white. "Fifty thousand?" Nash echoed. "If they are already at Lange, it will only take them a few days to get here."

Rhia nodded grimly. "It sounds like they intend to bypass the mountains farther south, where they are engaging us with another force." She scowled. "With so much of our own forces concentrated there, the Zallabarians will be able to go take Zuar City before we can come back to intercept them." The shock and horror on her and Nash's faces told me they understood exactly how devastating that would be.

"We might be able to stop them if we can convince the general to send the bulk of our dragon riders this way," Nash pointed out.

"But how long will it take us to get to the general and convince him?" I argued. "And will he even listen? With me being the only witness, it is far more likely that he will throw me back into a cage without bothering to hear my report," I added bitterly. "Besides, the number of dragons we bring won't matter in the face of the hundreds of cannons the army is hauling. We will just be putting them in unnecessary danger."

"You don't have to tell me that." Rhia shuddered. "One of our dragons at the border camp had his left wing shredded by a cannon. He was a bloody mess when he was hauled back to camp, multiple broken bones in his wings and ribcage. The healer was able to repair some of the damage, and his dragon healing will help, but it could be weeks before he fully recovers."

Ykos nudged Rhia's arm, and she twisted around to look at him, the two in silent conversation. *"I have been speaking with Ykos and T'augus,"* Lessie said, *"and the three of us think we would be better served flying ahead to warn Zuar City of the attack."*

I said as much to the others, and Nash frowned. "Zuar City is the likely target, but they are not the only ones who need to be warned. We also need to tell the camp here at the channel, and the one at the western border."

"We can do the channel camp now," I said, "but there is no time to do both Zuar City and the western camp together. We'll need to split up."

Decided, the three of us mounted up and flew the rest of the way to the camp. We landed directly outside the stables, drawing the attention of the watch. The stablemaster and several soldiers rushed up to meet us, their eyes widening in anger and amazement when they spotted me and Lessie with the others.

"Private!" the stablemaster called, jabbing a finger at Rhia. "What are you two doing, traveling with her? Are you aware that she's a prisoner, and supposed to be headed to the other camp to await court-martial?"

"She's not a prisoner," Rhia said coldly, "and we have more important matters to discuss. Where is the officer in charge?"

The three of us dismounted, and the two soldiers who'd

responded immediately started for me, hard glints in their eyes. They stopped short when Lessie snarled, and the other two dragons moved in, preparing to intercept if necessary.

"I'd stand back, if I were you," Rhia said, still using that same cool tone. "And alert whoever has been left in charge of our arrival."

"It's Captain Blaney," the soldier on the left said stiffly, eyeing the dragons with barely concealed anger. "We'll take you to him now."

The three of us were escorted to Colonel Roche's office, now manned by the captain. Blaney was a surly man with salt-and-pepper hair and a gut protruding from behind his uniform belt. With him were two dragon riders—one of the two pairs that had been left behind to help defend the camp.

"What is the meaning of this?" the captain demanded, his bushy brows drawn into a scowl. "I thought you were sent here to augment our dragon rider force. Why have you brought Kenrook with you? I cannot believe she would have already been pardoned."

"Never mind Zara's presence—there are more important issues to focus on," Rhia said, dismissing the captain's unspoken accusation with a flick of her hand. "We are here to warn you that a large force is on its way from Zallabar, by way of Dardil. We believe that they intend to strike at Zuar City while the bulk of our force is occupied at the western end of the border."

"And how do you know this?" one of the riders, a lieutenant, asked. His eyes glittered with disdain as he looked at me. "Why would any of you three have been sent to Dardil, when we are supposed to stay out of neutral territory?" I had the distinct sense that he and his partner were angry at being left behind here, away from the action, and hated the idea that the three of us, young upstarts in his eyes, had been in the thick of it.

"They weren't in Dardil," I said before Rhia could answer. "I was. I could waste time explaining why, but there's no time. Zallabar is sending fifty thousand men to attack the heart of the country, and we are *defenseless*. This is no time to be squabbling!"

The two riders exchanged glances, their expressions going vacant. I had the distinct sense they were communicating with their dragons, and I hoped our own dragons had relayed the danger to them. Lessie, despite her diminutive size, had a way of convincing other dragons to do what she wanted—back at the academy she'd practically run the show at the stables, and even here, where we were considered the enemy, she'd gotten a few of the dragons to side with her. I suspected it had more to do with the fact that she was female than anything else—with dragon numbers dwindling by the year, females were prized and very rare.

"Even if what you're saying is true," the captain growled, "there is nothing my men can do. There are only forty of us stationed here, not enough to make a difference against a force as massive as the one you described."

Nash gave the captain a look of pure contempt but held his tongue. I suspected that the captain and the other soldiers who had been left behind—riders notwithstanding—were either old or lazy, better suited to keeping a lookout on a backwater camp that had little chance of being attacked rather than being sent to the front. It was little wonder that the captain wasn't being particularly helpful.

"You may not be able to do anything, Captain," Rhia said, "but the riders who've been stationed here can help us spread the word."

"They've been ordered to—"

"We will help you," the lieutenant interrupted, addressing Rhia. The anger he'd directed at me earlier was gone, his face now set in grim but determined lines. "I will depart immediately for the western border to warn the general, and Durley"— he gestured to his partner—"can go to Zuar City to warn the council and the academy."

"Very well, but I think you should take Nash with you, since the route is more dangerous," Rhia said. I felt a surge of pride as I watched her take command of the situation—it was as if the captain didn't even exist. "Durley can go to Zuar City, while Zara and I stay behind to warn whoever is out on patrol of the impending attack. The four of us can spy on the advancing army, and once we can confirm their invasion and the direction they are headed, we can report that information to the general."

But I shook my head at that. "I would come with you if I was truly needed, but between the six of you everything is covered. Lessie and I aren't going back to the military until we get a fair hearing." Although I didn't know what I wanted to do, truthfully. Should Lessie and I try to follow that ferry and track Salcombe? The guard had given me a rough direction of where it was headed, and I might be able to follow without passing over Dardil, which was undoubtedly hostile territory now.

"Of course," Rhia said gently, giving me an understanding

look. The captain and the other two riders gave me disapproving looks but didn't say anything—I suspected they knew they couldn't enforce Colonel Roche's orders, and there were more important things to attend to, anyway.

Finished discussing the particulars, we went our separate ways. The other two riders headed for the barracks to pack their belongings while Rhia, Nash, and I went to the stables to check on our dragons. They were resting comfortably in their stalls, and the stablemaster had fed them. Full and exhausted from our travels, Lessie was passed out in her stall, snoring loudly as she lay belly up on her pile of hay. The sight made me smile, despite everything happening around us.

Once Nash and the other two dragons had taken off, Rhia took me aside so we could speak privately. "I'm so sorry things have turned out this way," she said as we walked along the tree line just outside of camp. "You and Lessie truly don't deserve the way you've been treated."

"Thanks." I swallowed against the sudden lump in my throat, exhaustion allowing my emotions to get the better of me. "I wish I could say that all of this is behind me now, but I know it's not. I'm going to have to face that hearing at some point, and if Tavarian doesn't come back, I'll be sent to prison for certain." *Why hadn't he come back?* I wondered, my chest tightening with anxiety. He'd promised he would. Perhaps he had passed by here and, noting that the camp was mostly abandoned, continued on. But I would have thought he'd at least check in at the camp before moving on, and the captain hadn't mentioned him.

Rhia sighed. "The truth is, you've been thrust into an impossible situation with insufficient training and supervision. Honestly, if Roche thought you were so untrustworthy and incompetent, she should not have sent you into danger. With everything that's happened, it's a wonder you're still alive."

"A testament to my skill and prowess?" I said, grinning.

Rhia smirked. "And maybe a healthy dose of good luck."

"In all seriousness, though, lack of training has nothing to do with it," I said. "After all the training Lord Tavarian gave me and Lessie, we were more than capable of carrying out the jobs we were given. If Roche hadn't been so prejudiced, and my superiors so set in their ways, things might have gone a lot differently. But," I added, forcing myself to let go of the resentment bubbling in my heart, "none of that matters now. Our country is about to be overrun by the enemy."

Rhia winced. "Is it really that bad?" she asked. "I know you said fifty thousand men and close to a thousand cannons, but is it possible you miscounted?"

I shook my head. "I know what I saw. Zallabar's weaponry is far superior, and our own country has grown sloppy and complacent in their mistaken belief that we're the most powerful country in the region."

"Too true," Rhia said, and I hated the hopeless look in my friend's eyes. "I wish there was something more we could do. You were able to convince Traggar to back down by knocking over the right domino. Isn't there anything similar we can do to get Zallabar to retreat?"

"Tavarian would know better than me," I admitted, and felt another pang of longing. Dammit, but I missed the man, even if he did drive me a bit crazy at times. "To be honest, my biggest fear is for the dragons. Yes, we will lose human lives in the war, but the Zallabarians are probably more interested in subjugating us than wiping us out. The dragons, however, they will kill without mercy."

"You're right." The color leeched from Rhia's face. "Zallabar will have no interest in taming them, even if they could. Wiping out the dragon race will prove to the world that Elantia has fallen once and for all, and that they are the new power to be feared in the region."

"Isn't there anything we can do about it?" I asked, that horrible image of Lessie's wings, shredded by cannon fire, rearing up in my mind again.

"I don't think so," Rhia said as we turned around, heading back toward the stables. "I don't want anything to happen to Ykos either, but this is the price of our privileges as dragon riders. In exchange for our higher status, we must be willing to sacrifice our lives, and the lives of our dragons, when necessary."

"I agree, but what is the point if we are going to lose anyway?" I argued. I would happily sacrifice my own hide, even though I'd never had much chance to enjoy the privileges Rhia spoke of, if it meant saving my country, but we were so hopelessly outmatched it seemed a fruitless endeavor. "Throwing away the lives of our dragons when there is no hope of victory is not my definition of 'necessary.' If we can't win this war, then at the very least we must fight to preserve the lives of the creatures who helped bring Elantia its glory and fame."

The sound of beating wings had Rhia and me looking up before she could answer. The other two riders who were out on patrol had returned, and I fisted my hands at my sides as I recognized Captain Fosse and his dragon, Mirn. Dammit!

"What's wrong?" Rhia asked.

"The dragon on the left, and his rider, used to be my patrol partners," I said. "He's the one who got me reprimanded for saving those sailors who were locked up in the cargo hold on their sinking ship."

"Oh, he's one of those, then?" To my surprise, Rhia smirked. "I bet he's just thrilled at being left behind."

That startled a laugh out of me, and suddenly I wasn't in such a foul mood. Fosse would have seen this posting as a punishment—he was as ambitious as they came, with no qualms about stepping on others to achieve his goal. That he was left behind to patrol the channel instead of being allowed to fight would chafe terribly.

"You have a knack for finding the silver lining in things," I said fondly.

Rhia smiled. "In a world where every third sentence spoken aloud tends to be a lie, humor is necessary to keep myself from seeing the worst in everybody." Her smile softened a little. "You're one of the few people I know who almost never lies, Zara. That's why I like you so much."

I opened my mouth to respond, but Rhia turned her attention back to the riders, quickening her pace to meet them. Truthfully, I didn't know what to say to that anyway. I'd completely forgotten that Rhia's talent was truth-telling—she could sense lies the same way I could sense treasure. Or was it the same way? Treasure tended to chime or ring when it was near, but for all I knew Rhia's sense was more like an alarm. Or maybe it wasn't a sound at all, but a feeling. Either way, it must be incredibly awkward to know every time someone was lying, even about the simplest things, and I was suddenly grateful that I didn't have such an ability.

We made it to the stables just as Fosse and his partner, a petite female with raven hair, dismounted. He smiled at Rhia, no doubt taking in her curvy figure and glossy chestnut hair, but his eyes widened with astonishment when he saw me.

"Kenrook!" His mouth bowed as he frowned at me. "Aren't you supposed to be at the western camp? Preferably in a cage?"

"I am no longer a prisoner," I said, figuring that Rhia would forgive me for the lie. Or was it a lie? After all, I wasn't behind bars. "This is Rhiannon Thomas, formerly stationed at the western border. The two of us are here to warn you of an imminent attack."

I briefed Fosse and his partner, Xima, on the incoming force from Zallabar. Xima looked concerned, but Fosse laughed in my face. "You can say what you want, Kenrook, but I refuse to believe that after everything you've done, Roche would trust you with such information. As for you," he said, turning to Rhia, "I've never met you, and for all I know you're an imposter."

"Fosse!" Xima sounded scandalized. "Surely these two wouldn't be walking around here, unmolested, if their claims were unsubstantiated. They must have given the captain proof."

"The captain is a lazy fool," Fosse countered.

"Enough of this," Rhia snapped. "There's no time to argue. Durley and Michel have already left for the western camp and Zuar City to warn the general and the council. We agreed that I would stay behind and help the two of you with reconnaissance so we can confirm where the invasion force is headed."

"We will do no such thing," Fosse said icily. "As the ranking dragon rider in charge, I forbid all of you from doing anything until I say otherwise. As for you," he spat at me, his gaze glittering with cold rage, "it is clear you cannot be trusted. I cannot believe you managed to convince two other riders to fly off to high command without waiting for my orders. I suspect Roche is right, and you are working with the enemy to try and sow panic and confusion amongst our ranks."

"Fosse," Xima said, speaking up after a long period of silence. I could tell from the way her eyes suddenly cleared that she'd been conferring with her dragon, and I hoped he'd confirmed my story with Lessie. "I understand you do not trust these riders, but if there truly is an invasion we can't afford to sit on our heels and do nothing. At the very least, we should fly east and try to confirm the existence of this army. If they should invade, and it was discovered that we did not lift a finger to help, we will likely be court-martialed ourselves."

Fosse scowled, but he seemed to take Xima's warning seriously. "Very well," he said. "We will fly out tomorrow after our dragons have had a chance to rest. In the meantime," he said, jabbing a finger at me, "we must detain Kenrook before she can cause any more trouble."

He took a step toward me, and Lessie chose that moment to barrel out of the stables, roaring with anger. I used the distraction to punch Fosse straight in the jaw. His head snapped back from the force of the blow, and he crumpled to the ground, unconscious.

*On the ground,* I thought, *and exactly where you belong.* The burn in my knuckles was nearly as satisfying as the sight of him laid low. I'd had more than my fair share of being pummeled, bullied, and intimidated these past couple of weeks, and it felt damn good to finally get some of my own back, even if Fosse was only a minor thorn in the grand scheme of things.

Ignoring Xima's gaping and Rhia's smirk, I stepped over the unconscious captain and went to Lessie. *"I know you're still tired,"* I said apologetically, *"but we can't stay here."*

Lessie huffed, nuzzling my side. *"As if I would want to stay with these people anyway. Let's grab my saddle before we forget it again."*

"Oi!" Two more soldiers ran up, their weapons drawn. "You can't just—"

I spun on my heel to face them. "Unless you want to end up like this guy"—I nudged Fosse's prone form with my boot—"back off. I've had enough of being ordered around by people who couldn't give a damn about my life or what I have to say." Dismissing them, I turned to Rhia. "Do you want to come with me?"

Rhia shook her head. "Someone has to keep a lookout if Fosse isn't going to do it himself."

"We're not all assholes around here," Xima said. "I'll go out on patrol with you. Fosse might outrank us, but we outnumber him." She gave her partner a disgusted look, and I wondered if he'd treated her like dirt as well.

"Great." Rhia smiled, then clapped me on the shoulder. "Now let's get Lessie saddled up so you can be on your way."

FIFTEEN

With Fosse knocked out, and since I was in no immediate danger of being arrested, I allowed Lessie to sleep a bit longer to recover her strength. She had been willing to scoop me up and fly out immediately, but her exhaustion was bone-deep, and I could feel how sore she was through the bond. Another hour or two of sleep would allow her to repair some of those overworked muscles, so I lay down in the hay with her and snuggled while she slept.

Despite her weariness, Lessie didn't stay down for long. A few hours later, she was nudging me awake.

*"Mmm?"* I stretched my arms overhead. *"What is it?"*

*"Mirn has informed me that his rider has awoken,"* Lessie informed me. *"We should get going now before he makes more trouble for us."*

Groaning, I stumbled to my feet, then made for Lessie's saddle, which we'd dumped in the corner. She was already wearing her harness, so it didn't take much time to get the rest of her tack on. *"Where are we headed from here?"* she asked as I tightened the straps. *"Do you want to continue the hunt for Salcombe?"*

*"No."* Tempting as it was, Salcombe had to take a back seat for now. *"I want to go after him, but Fosse's behavior reminded me of how complacent people can be even when someone is screaming in their face that danger is coming. I want to go back to Zuar City and warn our friends."*

*"Won't the authorities have warned them?"* Lessie asked as I led her out of the stable.

*"Not necessarily. They'll have received the warning, but until they confirm the information, they probably won't tell the general populace for fear of causing unnecessary panic."*

I swung myself up into the saddle, and Lessie raced through the stables and up to the edge of the small cliff just outside. With a mighty beat of her wings, we were in the air, and I clutched the pommel as we rapidly gained altitude. Rhia had found me a set of dragon rider leathers to wear, and while they didn't fit nearly as well as the gear I'd been forced to leave behind in Traggar, it helped keep me warm.

*I'm going to have to start all over again with the armor,* I thought morosely. Dragon riders decorated their leathers with scales from their own dragons—a custom that was as much for function as it was for fashion, as dragon scales were tougher than most human-made armor. I'd only had a few scales fixed to mine, but they had been precious, as dragons did not shed their own scales very often. It took years to create a full set, and I wouldn't be able to start again until I had new leathers commissioned. That is, if I returned to the military and managed to come out of the court-martial unscathed. Which was highly unlikely.

*That's the least of your worries,* I thought, and forced myself to put it out of my mind. I devoted much of the flight time to the problem of defending Zuar City. Lange had come up with a contingency plan, knowing it was possible they would be invaded, but I doubted Zuar City had done the same. If I got there soon, there would be enough time to convince the residents to take precautions, hide supplies, and prepare to fight back in whatever ways they could.

But what to do with Lessie? She was far too large to stay in the lower city, and I had no doubt Zallabar would target Dragon's Table first to take out any dragons that might be there. I hadn't seen any more of those airships, but it was possible they were sending those from another direction to attack the upper city. Since I was avoiding the authorities, Lessie would have to contact the dragons and order them to evacuate, if there were indeed any who hadn't already been deployed. Perhaps there was already some shelter outside the city set aside for just such a purpose.

*"There is no reason for me to turn tail and hide,"* Lessie argued. *"I am a dragon, not a coward. Surely there is some way to put my talents to use."*

I thought about it for a minute. *"Maybe you can help evacuate some of the orphans. We can use Tavarian's hidden valley as a refuge."* Although I'm sure he never intended Maravel Hall to be used for that purpose, I was certain he wouldn't mind. And if he did, well, he'd have to get his ass back here so we could argue about it, wouldn't he?

*"I'm sure the children would love that,"* Lessie said wryly, *"but it might not be safe for them. Perhaps we could steal an airship and use that to ferry the orphans while I carry supplies?"*

We flew for a bit longer, tossing ideas back and forth, then stopped for a rest in a pretty, park-like valley that offered a clean well for drinking and a well-stocked pond full of fish. I imagined the valley was part of some rich family's estate, but no one came out to stop us as Lessie refueled.

*Everything is so peaceful here,* I thought as I sat beneath a tree. The sun was shining, the air sweet with the fragrance of blooming flowers, and off in the distance, I could see farmers working the fields and orchards. The sight almost made me doubt my memories of the army heading this way. Could war and death really be looming so close with this pastoral scene in front of me?

*"I saw the army too,"* Lessie reminded me, nudging my elbow with her damp snout. *"They are only a week behind us, two at the most."*

Her sober voice grounded me, but it also dimmed the sunshine as worry settled on my shoulders once more. *"I wish I knew if our warnings have been delivered,"* I said as I stroked her head. Was anything being done to oppose the incoming army? Did these farmers know that their fields and orchards would be set aflame should the enemy pass through here? Several times, we'd seen dragons flying in the distance at great speed, possibly messengers or scouts, but we'd dared not hail them or get close enough for them to get a good look at who we were, in case they recognized us and knew we were mutineers.

When we finally arrived at the outskirts of Zuar City, it was late afternoon, the sun still shining overhead. *"You should stay here,"* I said as we alighted on some cliffs a few miles away. *"It's not safe for you to go in during daylight hours."*

*"If you are going, then I am going,"* Lessie said stubbornly. *"I thought I would be okay when I let you off at Lange the other day, but when the enemy nearly shot us down upon our departure, I realized I could have lost you then, too. We are not separating again, for any reason. You promised."*

*"So I did,"* I said with a sigh. Realizing there was nothing for it, I settled down with Lessie, and the two of us kept watch on the city as we waited for the sun to set. I saw no dragons coming or going from Zuar City, which hopefully meant the rider who had delivered the warning to the council was already gone. From this distance, the city seemed perfectly normal, but perhaps luck was on our side, and the citizens were taking precautions.

If not, they would be soon, I vowed.

The moment the last rays of sunlight disappeared from the horizon, Lessie and I took flight. On silent wings, we glided into Salcombe's old garden, which Lessie and I had agreed ahead of time was an acceptable place to wait. She would draw too much attention if she followed me around the city by flight, and she was far too large now to walk the streets behind me without damaging the buildings or accidentally trampling pedestrians.

*"Perhaps I was a bit too hasty in my wish to grow as fast as I could,"* Lessie said grumpily, *"for now I wish I was small again, so I could follow you everywhere."*

I smiled, patting her on the head. *"The grass is always greener on the other side, isn't it?"*

I bid Lessie goodbye, promising to check in with her regularly, then raced across the street and climbed the roof of the nearest building. The familiar feel of tiles beneath my feet was soothing as I raced across the rooftops, and I breathed in the scents and sounds of my city, happy to be home. As I suspected, everything looked exactly the same, which was both comforting and annoying. There were no barricades or trenches set up, no windows boarded up—or at least no more than usual—no sense of fear or anticipation. There was just the normal buzz of the city nightlife—music spilling out from open tavern doors and windows, the clop of horse hooves and the rolling of carriage wheels, the mingled laughter and conversation of men and women alike, interspersed with the occasional wail from a stray cat.

The noise lessened considerably as I approached the Treasure Trove, the shop I co-owned with Carina Fontaine. My steadfast partner and best friend, Carina had a head for finances and the blood for treasure hunting—though she didn't go out herself. Her father had been a treasure hunter, and she knew how to appraise art and artifacts nearly as well as I did. While my ascension as a dragon rider had brought our formerly struggling shop quite a bit of business, her skills and good business sense were the reasons the shop stayed open and thrived when it could have easily gone under due to her being overwhelmed. I was deeply grateful to her and owed her more than words could convey. The least I could do was come back to the city to make sure she stayed safe.

As I expected, Carina was still in the shop with Kira and Brolian, counting the day's profits and cleaning up. The sign on the door was flipped to closed, so I used my lockpick to open the door, then stepped inside and inhaled the familiar scents of leather, metal, and old parchment.

"Zara!" Carina dropped the pen in her hand—as usual, she'd been marking up the ledger—and darted out from behind the counter. Her chocolate brown eyes glowed with surprise and delight as she rushed toward me, her black-as-night hair pulled into a high ponytail that nearly whipped her brother in the face as she passed. I grinned as she threw her arms around me and squeezed me tight enough that I was amazed my head didn't pop right off my shoulders. "What are you doing here?"

"Oh, just popping in for a little visit," I said, not quite ready to break the spell. For a moment, anyway, I could pretend that this was a homecoming, that I intended to pick right up where I left off and continue running the shop with Carina. I would go back to the old days, where I spent half the month at the shop and the other half on expeditions, unearthing lost temples or diving beneath crystal-clear waters where underground grottos awaited.

But dragon riding hadn't been part of my old life, and neither had Lessie. And even though I hated this war, I hated Salcombe, and I hated the military, I still wouldn't give up my dragon for anything in the world.

"It's good to see you, Zara," Brolian said, sweeping me into a bear hug. He'd filled out some since I'd last seen him, his form broader and more muscular, and the smile in his eyes seemed genuine. "I'm glad dragon riding seems to be agreeing with you, considering it's my fault you've become one."

I laughed. "You look good," I said, stepping back to survey

him. His black hair, the same shade as Carina's, was thick and shiny, and he seemed lighter, less troubled, than the last time I'd seen him. "Full-time employment suits you."

"You could say that," he said, his dark eyes unconsciously flicking in Kira's direction. My eyebrows rose as a blush darkened her creamy complexion. Was there something going on between them?

"Have you and Lessie been pulled from active duty?" Kira asked before I could bring up the subject. Kira was one of the orphans we'd hired on, old enough at sixteen to be kicked out on the streets to fend for herself, but inexperienced enough that whoring and thieving had been her only options. She was fiercely loyal to Carina and me for sparing her from that life, and I hoped one day the shop would grow big enough that we could employ more like her. "I can't imagine why else you'd be back here already, now that we declared war." She glanced at my dragon rider leathers and the dusty uniform.

"Not exactly," I said, wondering where I should start. I frowned as I noticed the other orphans weren't here. "Where are Nate and Tiana?"

"Nate found a job apprenticing for a tinkerer and moved out," Kira said. "Tiana is living upstairs with me now, but it's her day off and she's staying overnight at a friend's."

"Oh." I was happy Nate had found work somewhere he could learn a new profession, but a bit put out Tiana was out so late. I hoped she really *was* with a friend, and not a john.

"Tiana's fine, and what she does on her own time is her own business," Carina said, reading my thoughts perfectly. She seized my arm and marched me to the stairs. "We have questions, of course, but they can wait until after you've eaten and changed. You look hungry and exhausted, and no offense, but that uniform could probably stand up straight without you in it."

I laughed and allowed Carina to herd me into my old apartment, where Kira and apparently Tiana now lived. I still had a few changes of clothes stored away, which I was more than happy to change into after a quick shower. Even though I was technically still part of the military, I felt like a bit of a fraud wearing the uniform of an organization I continued to openly defy.

Over sandwiches and tall glasses of milk, I updated Carina and the others on everything that happened. Carina was outraged over my treatment by the military, but I did my best to gloss over that, trying to get them to focus on the present danger. "I wish I could say I was exaggerating," I told them after swallowing my last bite of ham and cheese, "but everything I've seen indicates that the invaders will be here soon. We have to prepare."

Kira shook her head in disbelief. "I believe you saw what you saw, but how can you be certain they're headed here?" she asked. "And if everyone has been warned, is there really cause for alarm? Surely our military will defend the city, as they always have. And our dragons will stop the army with their fire before they get within striking range."

"No, they won't," I said, my voice hard. "The enemy has shrapnel cannons far superior to the ones they used in the last war and capable of destroying a dragon's wings. Even if we sent every last dragon we have from the western border, it won't be enough, and there isn't enough time to mobilize our forces and bring them back here to meet the Zallabarians. The battle at the border is just a distraction to clear the way for them to take the capital."

Carina raked a hand through her midnight hair. "It's all a bit overwhelming, to be honest," she said, staring blankly out the window. "We have the muncies, of course, and the upper city guard, but that's hardly enough manpower to stand against the army you described. None of us have any experience dealing with a situation like this. What do you suggest we do?"

"I'm not sure there's anything we can do to keep the city from being taken," I said bluntly. Kira and Brolian looked stricken at my words, but I didn't see any point in beating around the bush. "But we can protect ourselves at least. We should hide our more valuable stock in the underground cellar, and stockpile what food we can. Actually, scratch that last part —we should pack whatever we can carry and get out of the city entirely. I know a place we can hide that isn't too far," I added, thinking of the underground ruins of the city palace. With any luck there wouldn't be any more matchkins or other dangerous beasts hiding down there, and if there were, we'd be well armed this time.

Carina scowled. "I'm all for securing our valuables and stocking up on food, but I'm not going to run away," she said. "This is my home, and my business is here. I can't abandon it, and you shouldn't either."

Carina's words were like a slap in the face. "I'm sorry," I said as sharp pinpricks of guilt stabbed me. I'd had very little to do with the shop in recent months, and though Carina never complained, I felt terrible that I'd dumped the bulk of the work on her. "I guess I haven't been a very good business partner, have I?"

"Don't be silly," Carina said. "You've put your life on the line for this shop more than once, and without you, we would have closed a long time ago. I know you've been distracted by all of this turmoil," she said more gently, laying her hand atop mine, "but don't forget you have a home here, Zara, and that it's worth defending."

My throat tightened with emotion, and I battled against a sudden wave of tears. "That's why I came back, isn't it?" I asked, putting on a brave smile.

"Yes, and that's why we love you."

With that, Carina sent Kira and Brolian back downstairs to finish cleaning up, while she and I went down into the cellar beneath the shop to prep it. We spent hours cleaning out the dark, dingy place, then went back upstairs to finish cataloguing all new additions to the shop so we could determine what needed to be stored and what we would keep in the front. After all, the Zallabarians weren't arriving for at least a week, and we didn't want to clear out the storefront altogether when there was a chance we could make some coin.

"Speaking of coin," Carina said, pulling out a small but hefty purse. "Most of your share of profits is in the bank, but I can give you a portion now. You'll be needing it now that you're back."

I took the purse, feeling guilty all over again at the mention of my share. "You don't need to keep setting aside half for me," I said. "After all, it's not like I've been earning it."

"Again," Carina said calmly, though temper sparked in her

eyes, "the shop wouldn't be running if not for you, Zara. You'll take your fifty percent share, and I won't hear another word about it."

The fierce undercurrent in her voice sparked something within me, and I threw my arms around her in a sudden burst of emotion. "I love you," I mumbled into her hair. "You know that, right?"

"Yes," Carina said with a laugh, the tension vanishing. "Now stop being such a sap and help me out here."

We worked into the wee hours of the morning and then stumbled to Carina's house a few blocks away to catch a few hours of rest. I gave Lessie a quick update before I passed out on the guest bed.

When I woke up again, it was to find a note on the kitchen table, Carina nowhere to be found.

*Went out to get supplies,* the note read. *Leave a note if you're heading out before I get back.*

I washed up, grabbed some toast and jam from Carina's larder, then found a piece of paper and scribbled a note back that I was going out to check on Lessie. I found her exactly where I had left her. The remains of a sheep carcass were littered nearby.

*"Sorry,"* she said, though she didn't sound the least bit apologetic. *"I was hungry, so I went hunting."*

I wondered briefly if the farmer she'd stolen the sheep from would agree with Lessie's use of the term "hunting" in this scenario. Or had she snatched one from one of the livestock freighters at the docks? *"You could have woken me up if you were hungry,"* I said, a little grumpy. Lessie's coloring was very distinctive, and there was a good chance her theft would be traced back to me. *"I would have found a legal way to get you food."*

Lessie snorted. *"You needed your rest. Don't worry so much, Zara. Soon enough, a missing sheep will be the least of this city's worries."*

*"True."* I sat down next to her. *"So, where shall we begin?"*

After conferring with Lessie, I decided to make Salcombe's old residence my home. There was no need to impose on Carina when there was an entire house here; the way I saw it, Salcombe owed me after the hell he'd put me through, and his yard meant I could stay near Lessie rather than having to sleep all the way across town. The front door and most of the windows were still boarded up, but I used my lockpick to gain access through the outside entrance to the cellars, then went up the stairs and inside the house.

It was strange to be back here by myself, I thought as I walked through the darkened hallways and breathed in the musty air. It seemed half a lifetime since the day I'd come here asking Salcombe for a loan to help cover Brolian's debt to a local gang so Carina wouldn't be forced to sell her share of the shop. Instead, I'd been sent to Lord Tavarian's estate to steal the first piece of heart. Not knowing the importance of the object, and desperate for cash, I'd done what he'd asked, only to wind up with a newly hatched dragon.

*My life has changed in so many ways,* I thought as I picked up a vase sitting atop a side table in the hall. Tracing the blue vines that curled over the glossy white china, I recalled that Salcombe had brought the piece back from Ailand, a country in the far east. Most of the art and artifacts in the house came from an expedition, but this had been something I'd seen in the shop window, and Salcombe had bought it when he'd caught me admiring it. He didn't often show affection, but those small acts of kindness had kept me by his side for much longer than I would have stayed otherwise.

*I wonder if he was merely trying to manipulate me into thinking we had a bond, or if he genuinely cared,* I thought as I set the vase back down. It didn't matter now; he was my enemy, and we'd passed the point of no return.

Shaking off the old memories, I climbed up to my old tower room. It was a small room with a single mattress, a chest of drawers, an armoire, and a shelf that had once been filled with books and small finds that Salcombe had allowed me to keep as mementos from past expeditions. Most of the touches in this room that had made it mine were gone—even the bedding had been stripped—but I rummaged through the dressers and came up with the cloth cap I was hoping to find. I'd used it often during my thieving days to hide my distinctive red hair, and I did so now, bundling my hair into a knot at the top of my head and pulling the cap over it. The last thing I needed was for the muncies to give me a hard time—some of them might know I was a fugitive from the military and would be only too happy to haul me up to Dragon's Table, where I would be detained. Once my hair was secured, I left the house and headed to the market to gather the supplies I'd need for the next week.

It was time to get to work.

SIXTEEN

Since I couldn't go to Dragon's Table myself, I sent Lessie up on our second night in the city to warn any dragons who might be up there of the impending invasion. She reported back that four dragons were temporarily staying at the academy stables, but none in the city itself, and that all had taken her warnings seriously.

*"Actually, it turns out that they all know about the incoming invaders,"* she said as we curled up together in the grass outside Salcombe's house. The moon was a mere sliver in the cloudy night sky, making it almost impossible for anyone flying overhead to spot Lessie unless they were actively searching for her. *"One of them had just returned from scouting the army's progress. He destroyed a couple of bridges on the way back, which should slow the invaders down a couple of days."*

*A couple of days.* Not enough to turn the tide of the war, but better than nothing.

The next morning, I returned to the shop to meet Carina,

Kira, and Brolian. As I expected, the impending war had caused citizens to tighten their purses, and traffic was lighter today, enabling us to work on stocking the underground cellar. In between customers, Brolian and Kira continued to carefully pack and move pieces underground, while I went to the orphanage to enlist some extra hands. It didn't take much to convince Miss Cassidy, the orphanage mistress, to lend me a few of her older charges, especially when I flashed a bit of the coin Carina had given me. The four of us went to the market and bought a large supply of dried beans, grains, hams, and other long-lasting foods, which we laid in the orphanage's cellar. Prices were already beginning to climb, thanks to the rumors swirling about, but I managed to buy enough to last several months. The supply would hopefully feed not just Carina, myself, and the employees, but the orphans as well.

The volunteers, touched by our unexpected act of generosity, asked what else they could do to help. After a moment's thought, I gave them the rest of my coin and ordered them to use it to buy and distribute supplies to the poor families with children, and help them secure their homes if possible. Starvation was a city's greatest enemy during a siege...and although it might have been optimistic of me to assume we'd even last long enough to endure a siege, I still wanted to be prepared.

Once I had that sorted, I returned to Salcombe's house for a shower and to feed Lessie, then headed to bed early. The hot water helped ease my sore muscles some, but as I flopped onto the bed, my back throbbed in protest. The orphans had helped a lot, but I'd still had to pull heavy carts, lift large sacks of grain and beans, and shuffle various art and artifacts of all sizes as we struggled to fit as much food and supplies in the cellar as possible. We'd also had to smuggle in bricks and use them to wall off the supplies so that the invaders wouldn't be able to find them. Exhausted didn't even begin to cover it.

Lulled by the softness of my former bed—which was surprisingly comfortable despite its size—I drifted off to sleep. I wasn't sure how easy it would be to sleep in Salcombe's house, but Lessie's solid presence in the garden was reassuring. If anything happened, I could count on her to tear their heads off or char the flesh from their bones.

Who knew that the thought of something so violent could be so comforting?

"Zara." Lessie's voice tugged me awake. Part of me wanted to burrow into the pillow and go back to sleep, but the sense of urgency in the bond had me opening my eyes to check my watch. Two in the morning. "I think someone is in the house. I hear movement on the lower floor."

I bolted upright, completely alert, and slipped my feet into my spelled boots. Creeping to the door, I opened it, my dragon blade in hand. At first, I heard nothing, but as I crept down the winding staircase and through the hallway, I caught the faintest noise of someone rummaging through drawers. The sound grew louder as I rounded the corner, and I paused at the sight of the study door open, candlelight spilling onto the carpet. Could it be that Salcombe had returned? He'd taken all of his dragon lore books, and the city guard had confiscated much of his belongings, but many of his books remained in the house. Was there something of importance here that one of us had missed?

Steeling myself, I approached the open door, prepared for a

confrontation with my old mentor. But to my surprise, it wasn't Salcombe. A hooded figure stood behind the desk, but he was too tall, his shoulders too broad, and the way that he searched the drawers methodically, opening each one, told me he was not familiar with the space. I wondered how he'd gotten in without alerting Lessie.

A shadow moved in the window behind the intruder as Lessie approached the house, preparing to catch the intruder if he decided to escape through the window. The stranger closed the drawer, swearing softly under his breath, and I darted to the side so he wouldn't see me when he looked up. I held my breath as his footsteps approached, but they stopped before they reached the doorway. I peered around the door to see him scanning the shelves, as if looking for some hidden box or compartment.

He was so intent on his search that I was able to slip behind him easily and press the tip of my dragon blade into his back. "Turn around," I ordered. "Slowly."

The man did as I said, and I hid a gasp. It was Red Beard, the leader of Salcombe's dragon god acolytes! I'd last seen him in the catacombs beneath the death temple, performing some kind of ritual dedicated to the dragon god before he and the other acolytes had drunk the dragon heart elixir. In the light from the flickering lantern, I could see his face clearly—he was a pale-skinned man in his mid-forties, with a thick head of hair the same color as his beard. His hazel eyes narrowed in recognition as he studied my face.

"You know who I am," I accused, placing the tip of my blade

right above his heart. "Tell me who you are, and why you're trespassing in my home."

"Your home?" the man said in a haughty tone as he lifted his chin. "This house is the property of the city government, not some squatter. If anyone is the trespasser, it's you."

I opened my mouth to threaten him when he moved, his form blurring. Suddenly he was behind me, and I cursed, remembering the dragon god elixir gave him enhanced speed and strength. Spinning around, I chased after him just in time to see him disappear up the hall through an opening in the wall I hadn't known existed. I nearly reached the opening when it closed behind him, the edges of the door sliding so seamlessly into place that I wouldn't have known it was there if I hadn't seen it with my own eyes.

Cursing, I slid my hands along the wall, searching for the trigger mechanism. It took me nearly fifteen minutes to find it, and by the time I followed the tunnel, which led to a cellar beneath a general store a few blocks away, he was long gone. Furious, I retraced my steps back to the house, then went back to the study with a canvas bag in hand.

"What were you searching for?" I muttered as I emptied the contents of the drawers into the bag. I took the lot with me to my tower room and dumped it out on the bed, then sat cross-legged on the mattress to sort through it. But it was almost completely scholarly correspondence—the locations of certain manuscripts, bills for rare volumes, and so on. I assumed the city guard had already gone through all of this when Salcombe was first unmasked, and left it where it was, having deemed it as useless as it appeared.

*It can't all be useless,* I thought. *There must be something here.*

I finished going through everything and found only one item of interest: a short letter from a treasure hunter whose name I was vaguely familiar with, who had passed away a couple years ago. *Your hypothesis regarding the origins of the child checks out,* the letter read. *A full report will arrive at your doorstep, along with the bill, next week.*

I scowled, checking the date. It was written only a month after Salcombe had taken me in. The writer had to be referring to me, and yet why would Salcombe employ a treasure hunter to check into my background rather than a private eye? Or had this man been both? It wasn't the first time I'd heard of a treasure hunter moonlighting—not everyone was good enough to make a living at this. The letter was sent from Rovin, a small town in southwestern Elantia. Could that place have anything to do with my origins, or was that where this particular treasure hunter had hailed from?

Blood pumping, I rummaged through the letters again, searching for the report, then went back downstairs and tore the study apart. *Of course it isn't here,* I thought crossly, slamming a drawer shut with more force than I'd intended. Had Red Beard taken the report? But what would he want with such a thing? It was infuriating to think that the secret of my parentage had likely sat here for over a decade, just out of reach. I'd snuck in here countless times as a teenager and had never suspected.

"*At least you have one clue,*" Lessie said, trying to console me. "*Perhaps when this is over, we can go to Rovin and ask around. Surely there can't be that many dragon rider families living there if the town is as small as you say it is."*

"Maybe," I said, but I couldn't find it in myself to be optimistic. Rovin wasn't in the path of the invading army, but that didn't mean it was safe. What if the town was destroyed before I ever got a chance to visit?

Annoyed with my pessimism, I returned everything to its proper place, then began searching through the volumes on the shelves, hoping to find stray pieces of correspondence tucked between the pages of a book. I was so intent on the search that when Lessie called my name again, I barely heard her.

"ZARA!" Her voice reverberated so sharply in my skull that I was hit with an instant headache. *"The muncies, at the garden gate!"*

"Shit!" I dropped the book and raced up the stairs to my tower room. The front door banged open as I hurriedly shoved my meager belongings into a pack. I rushed to the window, unlatched it, then flung myself through and onto Lessie's back just as she passed below. From the alarmed shouts, I could tell that more than one of the guards had spotted her.

"Damn," Lessie growled, and I blinked—it was the first time I'd heard her swear. *"Where do we go now? I won't be able to stay in the garden any longer."*

I didn't answer right away, my mind racing to come up with a solution as Lessie pushed us higher into the clouds. Unfortunately, it was daylight now, and it didn't take very long before four large dragons surrounded us on all sides.

"Zara Kenrook," one of the riders barked, and I nearly fell off my saddle when I saw it was Major Falkieth. The other three were older riders I didn't recognize, likely from the reserves. "You are wanted by the state for treason, murder, and insubordination. Surrender now and return with us to Dragon's Table."

I swallowed hard, fighting against my natural instinct to rebel. *"The other dragons say that we were spotted by the lookout,"* Lessie said. *"They are sorry to have to do this, but they cannot go against their masters."*

*"I know."* I patted the side of her neck gently as I met Falkieth's gaze. "We'll come quietly," I said.

The four dragons escorted us back to Dragon's Table in silence. I tried to catch Major Falkieth's eye, but she wouldn't look at me. What did she think of me? Did she believe the charges? The idea that she thought I was disgraced struck me with a sudden sense of shame, and it took everything I had to stare straight ahead rather than duck my head. Major Falkieth had been one of my favorite instructors at the academy—as the dragon rider instructor she'd been no-nonsense but friendly, and a lot more practical than some of the other professors. The idea that she thought I was a traitor was almost more than I could bear.

The dragon riders brought us to the stables, where Lessie was immediately herded into a closed compartment. A pair of city guards were waiting, and for a moment, I expected them to drag me off to whatever passed for a jail in the upper city. Instead, they brought me to an underground room on campus that was not unlike my old dormitory room, except it was windowless with heavy bars on the outside of the door.

"You'll be kept here until your hearing," Major Falkieth said as I was ushered inside. Her weathered face was set in grim lines, her steely eyes unreadable. "The guards will escort you to the toilet when needed, but otherwise you are not to leave this room under any circumstances."

"Not even to see Lessie?" I asked, hating the note of desperation in my voice.

"Your dragon will be well cared for," was all she said.

"Please, Major Falkieth," I said, and started to explain, but she stepped back, and the guards shut the door. "Come back!" I shouted, pounding on the heavy wood until my hands ached. "I'm not a traitor! Let me out! I haven't done any of the things they've accused me of!"

But no one listened, and the tears that threatened finally spilled, carving hot, salty tracks into my cheeks. Sniffling, I swiped at them, then sat heavily on the edge of my bed. I'd been imprisoned before, back at the Traggaran jail, but even then, when I had been inches away from ending up on the gallows, I hadn't felt so low. But then again, it had only been my life on the line. Now it was my future, my honor and reputation. I'd done everything I could to help Tavarian, to stop Salcombe, to protect my country, and the idea of being remembered as nothing but a traitor and deserter was too painful to consider.

"*Zara,*" Lessie said softly. "*Are you okay?*"

"*Yes.*" I latched onto her voice like a lifeline—my only link outside these walls, though she was trapped too. "*Are you?*"

"*Well enough,*" she said, a hint of annoyance in her voice. But annoyance was much better than pain or fear, and I relaxed a little. "*They've fed me, and I've managed not to rip any heads off thus far.*"

I laughed a little. "*Please don't,*" I said. "*They're just following orders.*" The academy staff didn't deserve Lessie's wrath.

"*The other dragons are asking me questions about your upcoming court-martial,*" Lessie said. "*They are a bit skeptical, but I might be able to convince them of your innocence.*"

"That's great, but they're not the ones court-martialing me."

"*Still, if their riders can be persuaded to your side, that may work in your favor.*"

I paused, remembering Odorath, Major Falkieth's dragon. While she wasn't in charge, having her in my corner might be helpful. "*Fine,*" I said, flopping onto my mattress as exhaustion washed over me. "*Let me know if you make any headway, or if they tell you anything useful.*"

Knowing there was no point in torturing myself, I pulled the covers over my head and burrowed deeply. Maybe I could lose myself enough in dreams that when I woke up, I would find that this was all a terrible nightmare.

SEVENTEEN

If this was a terrible nightmare, it was a long, boring one. For three days I was kept in the underground chamber, let out only to relieve myself, my meals served to me with dull wooden utensils on wooden trays that were removed the moment I was finished with them. My belongings had been stripped from me once more, so there was no chance of either fighting or breaking my way out.

But if I was honest with myself, I was done fighting. I was done running. It was time to face the consequences of my actions, even if those consequences were unfair and unjust. I'd done everything I could to avoid this, and yet it was coming to pass anyway. I'd just have to present my case and hope for the best.

Though I'd—mostly—come to peace with my own ordeal, I was still anxious for news about the impending attack. Were the Zallabarians close yet? Was the western army racing back to defend the city? I'd pestered Lessie several times, hoping for answers, but she had little to say, and the guard who brought me my food refused to answer any questions.

Finally, on the morning of the fourth day, I had a visitor. "Major Caparro," I said as the headmaster walked into my room with my usual guard as an escort. "Good to finally see you." I kept my voice bland, hiding the burning resentment I felt. Why did he make me stew for three days?

"I'm sorry you've been kept waiting so long," he said, surprising me with the apology. "The war preparations have been taking all our time and attention, and I have had little free time to decide what to do with you."

"War preparations?" I pounced on the topic. "What news is there of the approaching army? I've been asking for days and no one will answer me."

"The Zallabarian army has been sweeping over the north almost unopposed," Caparro said heavily. "They are expected to reach Zuar City within the week at this pace. Even so, Colonel Roche is insisting on the court-martial. She has just arrived from the border on dragonback, along with General Sarte and several other high officers, to assist with the defense of the capital, so we have made time for the court-martial since the appropriate officials are here."

My heart leapt into my throat. "When is the hearing going to take place?"

"Tomorrow morning."

I swallowed against a sudden rush of nerves—this was all happening way too fast.

"Here," Caparro said before I could think of what to say. He handed me pens, ink, and a large sheaf of papers from a satchel he'd carried in. "Write down a detailed report of everything that has happened, and everything you have done, since you first arrived at camp. It will save us time."

I set the supplies on a small table next to the bed, then clenched my hands into fists in my lap to hide their shaking. "Anything else?" I asked as he rose.

"Get some sleep," he said before striding out.

The door closed behind him, the bolt slamming into place as the guard locked me in again.

I mulled over the encounter for quite some time after he'd left. Major Caparro hadn't been rude to me; in fact, he'd been unfailingly polite, and had even apologized, though aside from being confined, I hadn't been mistreated in any way. But neither had he been friendly. There was no way to tell how he felt about my court-martial, if he thought I was innocent or guilty, or if he was reserving judgment until the hearing. I didn't know how Major Falkieth felt either—she'd barely looked at me as she and the other riders had brought me in, but she'd treated me with her usual stern manner.

I reached out to Lessie and told her about Caparro's visit. "Good," she said, sounding much more optimistic than I felt. "It is about time that we got out of here—the Zallabarians will arrive any day now, and we cannot afford to sit around when we could be helping."

"Very true." I tried to smile, even though Lessie couldn't see my face, but I couldn't muster the effort. "I should start writing my report now."

"Take your time and make sure to include every detail you think will help our cause," Lessie said. "And don't lose hope," she added, reading my despair even though I tried to hide it from her. *"If the worst should come to pass, I'll break you out again and we will join Muza in his secret lair. It is far, far away from here—nobody will be able to find us."*

I hid a sigh at the childlike confidence in her voice. Times like this reminded me that for all Lessie's size, strength, and occasional glimmers of wisdom, she was still a baby. But just because I was miserable didn't mean I had to drag down her mood as well, so I let her have her optimism and turned my attention to the sheaf of papers on the table.

It took me all afternoon to write the report, and by the time I finished, the ground was littered with crumpled pieces of paper from sections I'd started and scrapped several times. I read the report three times, added a few more details, then handed it off to the guard when he brought me my evening meal.

The night brought little sleep. I spent most of it tossing and turning, agonizing over the report. Little details kept cropping up in my mind that I wished I'd added, and I questioned whether or not I should have scratched out certain sentences or even entire passages. That report was my only shot at freedom—if it wasn't sufficiently convincing, I would be thrown in a military prison, forced to rot there until I was old and gray. I harbored no illusions that Lessie would be able to break me free; I wasn't the first dragon rider to be sentenced to a lifetime in military prison, and I was certain there were protocols to keep Lessie from doing exactly what she had planned. They would likely sedate and chain her, as they'd done while I was trapped on Traggar.

A female guard awoke me early the next morning, with a

freshly laundered uniform in one hand, and restraints in the other. "Come on," she said after she bound my hands. "The headmaster wants you cleaned up before your hearing."

The guard escorted me to the bathing rooms, where I was allowed a quick shower and a chance to change clothes—the latter of which the guard had to help me with. The restraints were loose enough that I could give my hair and skin a good scrub. The hot water and soap washed away not only grime but also the layer of melancholy that had settled over my soul. By the time I emerged, I felt brighter, more alert. My stomach churned with anxiety now that the numbing despair had disappeared, but I forced down some porridge and tried not to think of the myriad of ways this hearing could go wrong.

Once I was dressed, my guard, along with three others, herded me into a brougham. I was expected to be brought to army HQ, but instead I was taken to the Dome of Justice, the government building at the center of town where all court proceedings were held. The silver dome glinted like a beacon in the morning light, and a white marble statue of a blindfolded woman in flowing robes graced the entrance. Her arms were extended at her sides, the right one lifted high as she held a feather in that hand, the left one dragging almost to her thigh, weighted down by a gruesome severed head. *Hephastia*, I thought numbly as we walked past her, *the ancient goddess of justice.*

My legs turned to jelly as they escorted me through the halls, but I forced myself to walk straight and tall. Just because I was being brought low didn't mean I had to let go of my dignity.

I'd done the right thing, and I would maintain that position to my grave.

I expected the staff to make me cool my heels in some waiting room for hours, but to my surprise, I was ushered into a small courtroom. Three rows of chairs were split down the middle to form a pathway to the front of the room, where a high bench loomed. Three of the five chairs were occupied by a stern-looking colonel, Caparro, and another major I didn't know. Two large desks faced the high bench, and a transcriptionist with some kind of typewriter sat at a smaller one off to the side. My stomach twisted at the sight of Colonel Roche seated at the desk on the right. Her expression was schooled, but I didn't miss the smug gleam in her eyes as our gazes met. I betrayed nothing of my own emotions as I was directed to sit behind the desk on the opposite side of the courtroom.

Silence descended over the chamber, punctuated only by the presiding colonel shuffling papers as he reviewed the case. I met Major Caparro's eyes, and my breath hitched as I caught a flicker of sympathy before he looked away. Did I have someone in my corner after all?

Finally, the colonel cleared his throat. A fourth man, who had been standing nearby, stepped up and ordered us to rise. He rattled off the details of the hearing in a brisk, no-nonsense voice. He announced the officers presiding over my hearing as Colonel Morel and Major Bernard, as well as Major Caparro. I gritted my teeth as the charges being brought were listed—treason, insubordination, murder, desertion, and a few others I wasn't even sure I understood. But it didn't matter, the message was clear enough—I was not only unfit for duty in the eyes of the military, but I was also an enemy of the state.

"Private Kenrook," Colonel Morel said when the man was finished. "How do you plead to these charges."

"Not guilty."

"Very well." He turned to Colonel Roche. "What evidence do you have to substantiate the charges you are bringing against Kenrook?"

Colonel Roche clasped her hands behind her back. "Sir, as detailed in my report, Kenrook is willfully insubordinate. She has defied her superior officers multiple times while out on patrol, risking both her life and the life of her partner to save a few stranded pirates on a sinking ship—"

"Pirates?" My blood boiled at the outright lie. "They were law-abiding Elantian citizens, and they—"

"Silence!" Morel barked. "You will not interrupt, and you will speak only when spoken to. Is that clear?"

"Yes," I said through gritted teeth, clenching my hands behind my back. I wanted to plow my fist straight through Roche's smarmy face, but all I would gain would be short-lived satisfaction, and probably another decade added to my sentence.

"Good." He turned back to Roche. "Continue."

Roche went on to paint a truly villainous picture of me. She claimed that Carvis was a seasoned, intelligent rider, and would never have flown into that storm of his own volition. More than likely, she claimed, I had deliberately drawn him into it so I could kill him and return to the enemy. I'd then sent my dragon back to the mainland so she wouldn't interfere when I joined up with my old mentor, Salcombe, who was likely a Zallabarian spy. Then, when the Zallabarian-Traggar alliance fell through, I must have called Lessie back to help Salcombe and me flee the country. She was convinced we went to Dardil to do more informant work for the military before the Zallabarian army came through.

"It's a good thing Lieutenant Jallis and his team managed to bring Kenrook in when they did," she finished. "This Salcombe character might have convinced her that consorting with the enemy was more attractive than serving her own people, but I'm sure the Zallabarians would have relished the chance to shoot Lessie out of the sky. Kenrook is a danger not only to herself and to the military but also to her own dragon. She must be put away for her own good."

"This is all well and good," Major Caparro said, "but I must point out that there is no evidence that Salcombe is a Zallabarian spy. He is a criminal, certainly, but all the intelligence gathered by the city guard on him suggests that he operates independently and has no allegiance to anyone but himself."

"Fine," Roche said, "but the rest of the timeline and facts line up." She shot a triumphant look my way. "My version of events is far more plausible than whatever story Kenrook has concocted."

I locked every muscle in my body down tight at the taunting undercurrent in Roche's words. She wanted me to lash out, to show the officers that I was violent and out of control and every bit as insubordinate as she claimed. Instead, I stared straight ahead and said nothing, waiting as the officers bent their heads and whispered amongst themselves.

Finally, Colonel Morel turned to me. "We have read your report, Private," he said gravely. "It is very detailed, and does coincide with quite a few events that our own intelligence agents have confirmed. But so does Colonel Roche's version of events. Why should we believe you over her?"

I met his gaze squarely. "Because I was there, and she was not."

The three officers questioned me at length about my report, making me go over several details again and again, challenging me to see if I could stick to the same story. "Her story is quite compelling," Caparro said, "and everything she's told us has been borne out by her dragon, Lessie."

"Excuse me," Colonel Roche said before one of the other officers could respond, "but are you really going to take the ramblings of a mere animal into account?" Disdain dripped from each word, so viscous I could practically taste it.

The other officers stiffened. "Are you implying that dragons are no more intelligent than the average beast of burden?" Colonel Morel snapped.

Colonel Roche paled, as if she'd realized her mistake. "I merely mean that the dragon is biased," she backpedaled. "Of course her account is going to match her rider's. The two of them can communicate telepathically, read each other's minds!"

A heated discussion ensued between Colonel Roche and the presiding officers. Major Caparro defended me, claiming that this hearing had been put together far too quickly, without the chance for either party to gather a list of witnesses, and that they couldn't possibly make a decision with such blatant lack of evidence. Colonel Roche insisted that the deaths of Carvis and Hallus were evidence enough, and in wartime they could hardly afford to have a murderer and a traitor amongst their ranks.

"Colonel Roche is right," Major Bernard said, and my stomach, which had been remarkably steady throughout the hearing, began to churn again. "It's not as if we have the luxury of peacetime, where we can easily gather the witnesses together. We only have the accounts of the parties involved to go on."

"That's right," Colonel Roche said, confident again. "Any witnesses will have been deployed by now and cannot easily be recalled to attend to this matter."

"Are you saying that—"

The rest of Major Caparro's outraged statement was cut off as the doors to the courtroom crashed open. Giddy relief rushed through me as Lord Tavarian strode in, silver eyes blazing. He wore a black coat over his tailored gray suit and black shoes, and though they were dusty with travel, the stains didn't detract from his commanding presence one bit.

"What is going on here?" he demanded, pinning Morel with a cold stare. Strands of midnight hair had worked their way free from the queue at the nape of his neck to frame his angular face, making him look wild. A thrill raced through my blood as I stared at him—he looked ready to do battle, and on my behalf, no less!

"We are conducting a court-martial on a soldier under my command," Colonel Roche barked, "and you have no right to interrupt—"

Tavarian spun and raked her with a look that would have

flayed the skin from most men. "I am Lord Varrick Tavarian, of House Tavarian," he said in a voice like thunder. "Zara Kenrook may have served under your command, but she is of House Tavarian as well, and therefore *my* responsibility." Dismissing her, he rounded on Colonel Morel again, who had gone white as a sheet. "Why is Private Kenrook facing this hearing alone? She has the legal right for a representative of my house to defend her, and at the very least a member of my household should have been contacted so counsel could have been procured. Did you ignore protocol because you incorrectly assumed she was not from a prominent family?"

"I—" Morel paused, clearly thinking better of what he'd been about to say, and cleared his throat. "Of course we know she is of your house," he said weakly, "but in wartime, legal niceties cannot always be observed, and there was no way to contact you."

"I am here now," Tavarian said, "and I can vouch for her story."

"You haven't even heard her story," Major Bernard protested.

"I don't need to," he said, and those simple words warmed me from the inside out. The knot in my chest loosened, and I took a full breath for the first time since the hearing started. "Private Kenrook was held in Traggar under duress by the criminal known as Salcombe, who was forcing her to help him retrieve a powerful magical artifact directly linked to the dragon god, Zakyiar." He ignored Colonel Roche's snort of disbelief. "Despite being under extreme duress, Zara was resourceful and quick-witted enough to orchestrate a fight between the

Zallabarian ambassador and the Traggaran king that ultimately resulted in the dissolution of the pending alliance between their countries. Through her actions, she has saved thousands of lives. She is a war hero, not a criminal."

The presiding officers bent their heads together, muttering amongst themselves. The triumphant gleam in Major Caparro's eyes, coupled by the fact that he alone had shown no surprise when Tavarian had stormed in, gave me pause. Had he known Tavarian was coming? If so, why hadn't he given me any warning?

"Officers," Tavarian interrupted after less than a minute had passed. "Are you questioning my testimony?"

"No, of course not," Morel said. "Your word is above reproach, Lord Tavarian. It's just that—"

"Then this hearing is over," Tavarian said. "It is illegal anyway and, unless you have any evidence to either refute my testimony or prove any of Colonel Roche's claims, is a waste of all our time. I insist that you remand Private Kenrook and her dragon, Lessie, into my custody until further notice."

"I concur," Major Caparro said. "This hearing can be postponed while Kenrook secures proper representation and until both sides are allowed time to obtain proper evidence."

"Very well," Morel said, albeit reluctantly. "Let the record show that Private Kenrook has been remanded into Lord Tavarian's custody and will remain there until after the Zallabarian invasion has been dealt with and we can reschedule."

"Excellent." Tavarian offered me his arm, his stone-like expression betraying nothing. "Come, Zara."

I took his hand and tried not to grin as we passed Colonel

Roche. Her face was beet red, and she looked like she was trying very hard not to screech at the top of her lungs. If she held it in any longer, steam would billow straight out the top of her head. As we walked out of the courtroom, I was surprised to see Major Falkieth in one of the chairs toward the back. There had been a half dozen people seated in the gallery when I'd arrived, but I didn't recall seeing her there. Her steel-colored hair was windswept, and she wore dragon rider leathers. She smiled as I passed, and that gesture of kindness loosened the last bit of my control. A huge grin spread across my face, and I actually whooped for joy as we walked into the hall.

"Try to show a little dignity," Tavarian said dryly as we exited the building. But there was a twinkle of amusement in his eyes as he glanced at me, and he squeezed my arm as if he secretly felt the same way.

"I have plenty of dignity," I said haughtily as we walked out into the sunshine. Gods, the sunshine! The sky was clear, the clouds were fluffy, and the scent of freshly baked pastries teased my nostrils, a faint whiff from a bakery a block or so away that made my stomach rumble. *I could eat,* I thought, but that had to wait. My dragon came first, as always.

Tavarian hailed a hansom cab, and we went straight to the academy to retrieve Lessie. The stablemaster, upon seeing Tavarian, released her immediately, and she bounded out of the stables and arrowed straight toward me.

*"You did it, Zara!"* she crowed as she pranced around us in a circle. Her eyes blazed with joy, and my mouth dropped open when she came right up to Tavarian and wrapped her foreleg around him in a hug. Tavarian gave a startled laugh, but he took

it in good humor and patted her neck. *"Tell Tavarian his assistance is greatly appreciated, but in the future, he should restrict this tendency for being fashionably late to less dire circumstances."*

I relayed Lessie's message, and he snorted.

"I came here as fast as I could," he told her. "It was a miracle I made it before the hearing ended, in fact."

I was about to ask Tavarian how he knew about the hearing when Major Caparro strode up to us, a leather-wrapped bundle in his hands.

"Your effects," he said, handing them to me.

"Thank you." I confirmed with my treasure sense that everything was there, including my dragon blade, boots, and lockpick. I glanced at Caparro and Tavarian, not missing the look that passed between them. "Did you know Lord Tavarian was coming?"

Major Caparro smiled. "I received word that Lord Tavarian was returning from Traggar and had been sighted at Port Lorring," he said, referring to a port town west of here. "After reading your report, I sent Major Falkieth there last night to fetch him, knowing the other officers weren't likely to give credence to your account."

"Then I thank you doubly," I said, with feeling. "If you hadn't intervened, I'd be on my way to prison right now."

"Indeed," Tavarian said. He smiled, clasping arms with the headmaster. "I suppose this makes us even now, old friend."

Caparro's eyes twinkled. "I'd like to think so."

"Old friend?" I asked, looking at them in an entirely new light.

"We served together, once upon a time." Tavarian offered no further explanation, holding his arm out to me instead. "Let's go home, shall we?"

*Home.* The word had never sounded as good as it did now. "Let's."

EIGHTEEN

As it turned out, "home" was Tavarian's floating island, which had drifted close enough to Dragon's Table that we could see it from the academy. Declaring it would be faster than those "cumbersome airships," Lessie offered to ferry me to it, then come back for Lord Tavarian. Tavarian was a bit surprised at the offer, but graciously accepted. It was quite an honor for a dragon to allow anyone other than their rider to mount them alone, but then again, Tavarian had just saved our lives. And Lessie had always liked him, even when I'd had my misgivings.

As Lessie and I flew to the floating estate, my thoughts drifted to Jallis. Things had changed quite a bit since he'd taken me on that first dragon flight. I wondered where he was now, if he was fighting at the western border, or if he would be sent back to Zuar City to help defend it. I hadn't seen him or Rhia at the hearing, and I was sure they would have come if Colonel

Roche had brought them with her to Dragon's Table. I hoped she had brought a contingent of riders with her and the general to help defend the city, or that they would be following behind.

Lessie dropped me off in front of the mansion, where I was greeted by Mrs. Durand, Tavarian's housekeeper. To my surprise, she greeted me warmly and brought me inside for tea while she prepared lunch. She served it with a small platter of biscuits, which I devoured as I paced the room, waiting for Tavarian and Lessie to return.

Thirty minutes later, Tavarian walked in, looking tired but satisfied. "Miss Kenrook—"

I threw myself at him before he could finish the sentence. "I have never been so glad to see anyone in my life," I choked out, tears spilling down my cheeks. Squeezing him tight, I sucked in a shuddering breath and inhaled a lungful of his scent—bergamot and leather layered over something else that was purely masculine and surprisingly appealing. His solid warmth was reassuring, a balm to my raw nerves.

Tavarian gripped my shoulders, pulling me back so he could look down at me with those molten eyes. "I wholeheartedly concur," he said, and suddenly he was kissing me, those full, soft lips meshing against mine. My mind froze, but my body responded instinctively, twining my arms around Tavarian's neck and kissing him back enthusiastically. Strong arms banded around my torso, crushing me against his solid chest. His heart pounded against my skin as he kissed me with desperation, with relief, with a joy that blazed through every single part of my body, and I poured all of those emotions and more into the kiss as I clung to him. It was a kiss that not only stole my breath completely but also made me question whether breath was truly necessary in the presence of such passion.

*Passion?*

The word echoed in my head, and it was so incongruous with Tavarian that I sprang away, the spell broken. "Sorry," I said, my cheeks blazing with embarrassment. "I uhh...got a little carried away."

"I believe we both did," he said, smiling. The warmth in that simple curve of his mouth, in those gleaming silver eyes, flustered me, and I looked away, finding the carved mantel very interesting all of a sudden. What was wrong with me? I wasn't exactly an innocent maid, and yet I felt like a teenager again, caught up in the excitement of my first crush.

*Get a grip, Zara.* I forced myself to meet Tavarian's gaze and bristled when I found his eyes twinkling with amusement. "What's so funny?" I snapped.

"Nothing." But his smile widened.

*Men.* They were impossible creatures, I decided, and promptly changed the subject. "Are you going to grin at me, or are you going to tell me what happened after we last spoke?"

His grin vanished, and I almost wished I hadn't spoken. Tavarian smiled so rarely, and these brief glimpses of joy transformed his face, giving me a glimpse of the man behind the stoic façade he so often wore.

"The morning after your court presentation, I reached out to the king's office and requested a meeting," Tavarian said as we finally sat down. "He agreed to receive me the following week, and I got him to promise to remain neutral by bribing Lady Hariana with a set of emeralds."

"Typical," I said, remembering how she'd flaunted the Traggaran crown jewels around her neck.

Tavarian smiled faintly. "I wasn't there in person when the jewels were delivered to her, but they clearly made the right impression, as it took no time at all to get the king to agree. I also reached out to the local papers, as I mentioned I would when we last spoke, and they published every word General Trattner said to you about the king that night, plus some embellishments. The Zallabarian ambassador has been mocked up and down the Traggaran coast and had no choice but to leave the country with his entourage on the first available ship."

"Wow." I sat back in my chair. "It was that easy?" *Of the two of us, I'd definitely received the short end of the stick,* I thought grumpily.

"Well, the military and navy tried to reverse the king's impulsive decision, but Zoltar had already publicly committed himself, so he was forced to uphold his decree. The fact that he received a very rude letter from General Richstein, the new Zallabarian dictator, may have helped things along," he said, and I was treated to another brief grin. "That letter was also mysteriously leaked to the press."

I laughed. "You are very good at your job," I said admiringly.

"It pays the bills," he said, and I snorted at the uncharacteristic sarcasm—he was independently wealthy and had no need to work. "In any case, the mood in Traggar had turned completely against Zallabar by the time I finished. I was about to head home, feeling quite good about myself, when I received

word that the Zallabarians had seized northern Elantia. I immediately diverted my ship to the west, and as you know, the rest is
history."

That explained why Tavarian had taken so long. Damn
King Zoltar for taking so long to receive him! "I suppose it's
lucky you decided to head straight for Zuar City instead of the
camp to check on me," I said. "Otherwise you wouldn't have
made it back in time for my hearing."

"Indeed."

A servant bustled in to announce that lunch was ready, and
we retired to the back garden to eat in the sun.

"Now it's your turn to fill me in," Tavarian said.

I gave him a rundown of everything that happened from the
time Salcombe had taken me to visit Lord Fanuel, all the way up
until Jallis and the other riders had captured Lessie and me.

"Lessie and I were so close to getting Salcombe," I said
bitterly as frustration kindled in me all over again. "He knocked
me out, but I'm sure she would have gotten him if Jallis and the
others hadn't caught up to me. And now he's off to who knows
where with two pieces of the heart in his possession."

"That is unfortunate," Tavarian said gravely. "I am truly
sorry you've suffered such mistreatment at the hands of the
military, but now that you are back in my custody I'll pull whatever strings necessary to ensure you won't be hampered by
them again. As soon as we have figured out what to do about the
invasion, we will focus all our efforts into apprehending
Salcombe."

"But what if he already has the other pieces by then?" I
asked desperately. "If he summons the dragon god, we won't be

dealing with an invasion anymore. We'll be dealing with the extinction of all life on this planet!"

"He will have to go through me to get the final piece," Tavarian reminded me. "Dealing with Salcombe is vital, but it is impossible to give him all our attention while our own country is being overrun. The cities to the north are already under Zallabarian control, and they are taking more territory every day."

My gut twisted as I recalled the might of that army. "How bad is the damage?" How many thousands had been killed because of Elantia's insistence on clinging to the old ways?

"The scouts report that the Zallabarians are not killing the civilians," Tavarian said, and I sighed in relief. "However, they are surrounding each city with cannons and confiscating supplies and food stores. That would be bad enough, but I am also concerned about our dragon rider forces. Colonel Roche brought ten riders with her, but many more should have returned from the western border by now."

I gripped the arms of my chair. "Where do you think they are?" I thought of Jallis and Rhia again. Were they all right? I couldn't bear it if anything happened to them or their dragons. I wished I could snatch them up and hold them close to my chest, out of harm's way. Maybe we could retreat to Tavarian's hidden estate and wait out the entire war there.

*"That would be selfish."* Lessie's voice intruded on my thoughts.

*"I know."* I sighed internally. *"It wasn't a serious thought. I haven't come this far just to dig myself a hole and hide."*

"I don't know," Tavarian said, bringing me back to the

conversation, "but I will be asking the general at the first opportunity."

"Is there anything Lessie and I can do to help?" I asked. I didn't know how we could beat back the invasion, not when the odds were so woefully stacked against us, but if the Zallabarians had to be dealt with before we could address Salcombe, I would throw everything I had into the effort. I knew it was silly, but Tavarian's reappearance had renewed my hope. Surely if the two of us could convince an entire nation to back out of a war, we could find a way to thwart a second nation.

"I wish we could get Zallabar to retreat with a few well-placed words," Tavarian said, and I realized I'd spoken that last part aloud. "But the time for diplomacy has passed, at least for now. We must find a way to strengthen our manpower and defenses before the enemy arrives."

I wracked my brain, trying to think of something, anything. "What about the floating islands?" I asked as a wild idea came to me. "Is there any way to steer them so they can be used to transport large numbers of men?"

He drummed his fingers on the arm of his chair, his brow creased in thought. "The floating islands could be a valuable resource, since they fly higher than the cannons can reach and are too thick for cannon fire to penetrate from beneath. Unfortunately, they can only be steered so far off their course, and the ones that would pass by the western border are too slow to make any difference. We could use them to evacuate, however."

"Or maybe for offense," I said, thinking of the cannon we'd salvaged from the airship that had attacked us outside of Zuar City. "Has any progress been made with that cannon prototype?

If we can replicate enough of them, we could mount some on the islands."

"I'm not certain," Tavarian said. "That's another thing I'll have to check on. But if not, we may be able to steal some of the enemy cannons and outfit my airships."

"How many do you have?"

"Three."

"Hmm." I did some calculations in my head. "With the amount of territory they've taken, the Zallabarians will have left maybe a quarter of their forces behind. That helps us a little, but ten dragons and three airships won't be enough. We need to find out how many troops, if any, are stationed here." I imagined that some soldiers would have been left behind, much like the skeleton crew that had been stationed at the channel camp. But the captain had told me there were only forty or so men under his command, and that was nothing in the face of an army that was close to forty thousand strong.

"*Zara,*" Lessie said, butting into the conversation once again. "*I think we should seek out the missing dragons. It's possible they've run into some trouble, and that some may have been killed. If we can find and rescue them, we might be able to hold off the enemy until our troops arrive.*"

I relayed her suggestion to Tavarian, and to my surprise, he agreed. "Rest up while I confer with the general and the council," he said, pushing back from the table. "If I have my way, we'll be leaving tonight."

Tavarian left to go work his magic, and I headed to my old room, the one Lessie and I had been locked into overnight all those months ago after he'd caught me trying to steal from him. I was pleased to see the housekeeper had sent my belongings up. A note on the vanity mirror said to check the drawers, and in them I found a collection of blouses, leather trousers, corsets, and other wardrobe essentials—all in my size and to my taste. I also found several coats and jackets in the closet, as well as packs and a few pieces of luggage. Tavarian couldn't possibly have had time to purchase new outfits for me upon arriving, which meant he must have stocked the room anticipating I would use it again someday. I wasn't sure how I felt about that, but Tavarian could more than afford it, and at this moment I was grateful for the assistance.

*I'll have to send word to Carina that I'm leaving again,* I thought as I packed a bag. She would be furious when she heard, but strangely enough, I was looking forward to the journey. I'd just returned from a harrowing journey, but knowing Tavarian and Lessie would be coming with me put me at ease. I hadn't asked for any part of this war, but if I was going to fight it, I could think of no better company to do so with.

Now, we had to figure out how to survive it.

*To be continued...*

Zara and Lessie's adventures will continue in War of the Dragon, Book 4 of the Dragon Riders of Elantia series. Make sure to join the mailing list so you can be notified of future release dates, and to receive special updates, freebies and giveaways! Sign up at www.jasminewalt.com.

Did you enjoy this book? Please consider leaving a review.

Reviews help us authors sell books so we can afford to write more of them. Writing a review is the best way to ensure that the author writes the next one as it lets them know readers are enjoying their work and want more. Plus, it makes the author feel warm and fuzzy inside, and who doesn't want that? ;)

# ABOUT THE AUTHOR

NYT bestseller JASMINE WALT is obsessed with books, chocolate, and sharp objects. Somehow, those three things melded together in her head and transformed into a desire to write, usually fantastical stuff with a healthy dose of action and romance.

Her characters are a little (okay, a lot) on the snarky side, and they swear, but they mean well. Even the villains sometimes. When Jasmine isn't chained to her keyboard, you can find her practicing her triangle choke on the mats, spending time with her family, or binge-watching superhero shows. Drop her a line anytime at jasmine@jasminewalt.com, or visit her at www.jasminewalt.com.

ALSO BY JASMINE WALT

**Of Dragons and Fae**

Promised in Fire

Forged in Frost

**The Baine Chronicles Series:**

Burned by Magic

Bound by Magic

Hunted by Magic

Marked by Magic

Betrayed by Magic

Deceived by Magic

Scorched by Magic

Fugitive by Magic

Claimed by Magic

Saved by Magic

Taken by Magic

**The Baine Chronicles (Novellas)**

Tested by Magic (Novella)

Forsaken by Magic (Novella)

Called by Magic (Novella)

**Her Dark Protectors**

*Written under Jada Storm, with Emily Goodwin*

Cursed by Night

Kissed by Night

Hidden by Night

Broken by Night

**The Dragon's Gift Trilogy**

*Written under Jada Storm*

Dragon's Gift

Dragon's Blood

Dragon's Curse

**The Legend of Tariel:**

*Written as Jada Storm*

Kingdom of Storms

Den of Thieves

Made in the USA
Coppell, TX
05 September 2023

21221327R00150